RECKONING
AT HARTS PASS

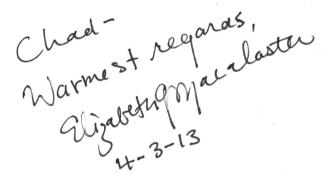

Chad —
Warmest regards,
Elizabeth Macalaster
4-3-13

RECKONING
AT HARTS PASS

A N O V E L

Elizabeth G. Macalaster

Reckoning At Harts Pass

ISBN: 978-0-9886992-0-5

Elizabeth G. Macalaster
PO Box 266
South Newfane, VT 05351

Cover photo by Dan Fenn
Cover and text design by John Reinhardt Book Design
Technical Editor, Daniel K. Sayner
Edited by Pamela D. Greenwood and Elizabeth Peavey
Copyedited by Bronna Zlochiver

Printed in the United States of America

To those men and women of the FBI
who work hard each day to keep our country safe.

ACKNOWLEDGMENTS

During the course of writing Reckoning At Harts Pass, family, friends, and readers offered ideas, encouragement, and inspiration. To them, many thanks: Dan, Jack, and Jane Sayner; Pamela Greenwood; Chad Basile; Mike Sweeney; Tom Redden; Amy Daniels; Dick Curtis; Peggy and John Martin; Lynn Franke and Jim Pierce; John Schlegel; Laura Wallingford-Bacon and Fred Bacon; Franziska Hart; Leslie Franklin; my southern family and friends: Lane and Frank Quinn, Peggy Burnett, Susan Bridwell, Mary Baysinger, and Peggy Powers.

Living well is the best revenge.

GEORGE HERBERT (1593–1633)

CONTENTS

xi

PROLOGUE

THE DENTED 1980 MERCEDES sedan sped across the flat Ukrainian countryside toward Hungary. It was 3 A.M., and the car's headlights cast long beacons into the darkness. Beyond the border slept the tiny Hungarian village of Béregsurany. Budapest lay just another 281 kilometers ahead.

The driver concentrated on the road, taking a long drag on his cigarette. He'd bought a carton of Camels, rare on the black market, and savored each smooth draw. His companion slept in the passenger seat. This had been an easy job—transport a box to a tailor in Budapest, pick up a couple of recently stolen cars, and drive them back to the Ukraine. Pretty routine stuff. Crossing the border at Beregsurany wouldn't be a problem. These days, guards looked for illegal immigrants trying to find a better way of life in Eastern Europe or for young girls kidnapped to supply the West's and Far East's desire for white, blond prostitutes. Besides, special arrangements had been made for them at the checkpoint.

The driver wondered what could be so valuable in the box tucked in his luggage. He and his partner worked as couriers for the Ukrainian black market and normally, they didn't know—or care—what they transported. But this time, their handlers seemed especially careful making the arrangements and were emphatic that the box reach Budapest.

He yawned. What the hell did he care what was in the box? He preferred to think about how he'd spend his share of the cut. Budapest was full of sex clubs yet untouched by the global recession. A thin smile stretched his lips. Maybe he could find one that offered a little something extra.

Just before the Beregsurany checkpoint, the driver shook his companion awake. At the gate, he stopped the car but kept the motor running. A uniformed guard walked out of the guardhouse and around to the driver's side. "Papers."

The driver rolled down his window and shoved their passports out. He lit another cigarette. The guard looked carefully at the passports, then at the men. He nodded toward the guardhouse.

"Open the trunk."

The driver saw two more guards walk toward the car. "What?"

"Get out slowly and open the trunk."

He'd been told there'd be no questions. No searches.

He glowered at the guard. "Just luggage in there."

The guard moved his hand toward the Glock pistol at his side. "I said open the trunk."

The driver slammed his foot on the accelerator. The Mercedes screamed forward, smashing through the gate. An alarm sounded.

His companion gripped the dashboard. "What the fuck are you doing?"

"Shut the fuck up," he replied. "We can't blow this."

"They'll kill us."

"Just shut up and let me drive."

From the side of the road, a large truck surged toward them. The driver swerved, but not in time. The truck rammed them, spinning the car around viciously. They dumped into a ditch.

The deputy commander of the border guards proceeded quickly toward the wreck. With him was a British diplomat from the embassy in Budapest. The deputy commander glanced at the unmoving thugs inside the car, then told his men to open the trunk. He rifled through the bags until he found what he was looking for.

He opened the box. Foam wrap cradled two small vials filled with a gray dust.

The diplomat pulled a cell phone from his jacket and dialed a number on the outskirts of London.

"Yes?"

"Sir, we've got the dirty package."

"Thank God," said the British intelligence supervisor, his voice filled with relief.

The haggard supervisor hung up the phone and gazed past the window at the rain drenching London.

"We caught it this time," he said to no one in particular. "Who knows about the next?"

PACIFIC CREST TRAIL

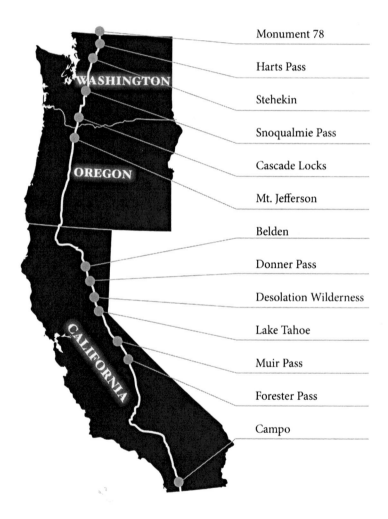

Monument 78

Harts Pass

Stehekin

Snoqualmie Pass

Cascade Locks

Mt. Jefferson

Belden

Donner Pass

Desolation Wilderness

Lake Tahoe

Muir Pass

Forester Pass

Campo

ONE

WHEN LUKE ROUNDED a bend in the trail and saw the bear cubs, his first thought was to simply leave the area. Unlike grizzlies, mother black bears weren't so adamant about defending their young, but still, he didn't feel a need to test that theory. During the past few weeks he'd managed to avoid bears. Stories from other hikers about bears creeping into campsites and snatching packs from under their sleeping heads were warning enough. He'd made sure he never pitched his tent where he ate or camped near any landmark named for the big pest. Bear Creek. Bear Lake. He walked right by. So far, it had worked.

Luke stood about 25 feet downwind of the cubs, which were nosing around a tree and hadn't smelled him. There was no sign of the mother, but Luke knew she was close. Slowly, he backed up, keeping his eyes on the cubs. The mother lumbered into view. He froze.

The sow stood on her hind legs and looked in his direction, sniffing the air. Her eyesight wasn't acute, but he knew she could smell better than a bloodhound. Although he was downwind of her, she detected him immediately. She snapped her teeth and exhaled loudly. Her cubs started up the tree.

Luke still didn't feel especially in danger—until he saw the wound on the sow's front leg. Either she'd been in a scuffle with another animal or had gotten the leg caught, perhaps in an old trap. Either way, it looked like it hurt and had put her in a foul mood. At six foot three inches, his pack extending another foot above his head, he might have looked like a large and foreboding four-legged creature to another animal. Even so, he'd be no match for an angry mother bear.

The hairs on the back of his neck rose. He was in trouble. And with few options. Running wasn't one of them. Moving at 30 miles per hour, the bear would be on him in seconds. Trying to climb a tree would be another mistake. The tall, sparsely branched spruces growing next to the trail offered no good foot- or handholds. Besides, bears can climb. Another option, the can of Bear-Be-Gone, was tucked into an outside pocket of his pack. His wife, Marina, had added it to his last re-supply box, insisting he carry it. But he'd heard the spray wasn't always effective. If it came down to it, it was better to fight a black bear.

It'd been a long time since Luke had had to face this kind of danger. He felt for the tomahawk tethered on his belt. For this journey, he had chosen to carry a steel Lagana Vietnam tactical hawk. Fourteen inches long, and barely a pound, it had served soldiers well from Vietnam to Afghanistan. Besides its use as a close quarter combat weapon, it was handier than a knife in the wilderness. Luke remembered the day he had finally learned the art of throwing a tomahawk.

*   *   *

"Let me see what you can do." Granddad stood a little behind Luke, his arms folded across his chest.

Luke turned and grinned at his grandfather. "I've been practicing."

Standing with his feet slightly apart, he lifted the tomahawk with his right hand, holding the handle as he would a hammer. He faced the dead stump, about 20 feet away. He breathed slowly, as his grandfather had taught him, and fixed his eyes on the stump. He raised his right arm over his shoulder, keeping the tomahawk's blade vertical. Stepping forward with his left foot, he threw, bringing the handle down to a near horizontal position, fingers spread open for release.

The throw was not hard, but it possessed speed and accuracy, rotating exactly twice before slicing one of three apples pegged in the center of the target stump.

Luke retrieved the tomahawk. Without looking at his grandfather, he took several steps backward from the initial throw point, aimed, and threw again. The tomahawk rotated three times and cleaved the second apple.

He pulled the hawk from the stump a second time and returned to where his grandfather stood.

"Now run," said Granddad.

Luke took off, running just to the left of the stump, and threw. The third apple broke apart.

With a trace smile, Granddad nodded and held out a package.

Inside was a ceremonial Chippewa tomahawk. The shaft was hollow, with a blade at one end of the poll and a bowl for tobacco at the other.

"You have learned well for your 14 years," said Granddad.

"Thanks, Granddad." Luke held the tomahawk in two hands, arms extended in respect.

* * *

HE STILL HAD THAT TOMAHAWK, tucked in a box at the back of his closet.

The sow dropped to all four feet. She continued to huff and slammed her good paw against the ground. Not a good sign. She lunged and then stopped—a bluff. She was less than 20 feet away.

Luke straightened himself as tall as possible. He avoided looking directly into the bear's eyes but talked softly to her. He tried to recall a Chippewa song Marina had learned from his grandfather's song book. When their girls were young, she had sung it to quiet them. "Hush, do you hear?" Then something about hearing loons…he couldn't even remember the tune, let alone the words. He took a couple of small steps backwards, fumbling with the buckles on the tomahawk's sheath.

Almost randomly, as if the idea were a second thought, the bear came at him. The ground shook under her weight. Luke ripped the Bear-Be-Gone from his pack and pulled the lever. She hit him.

Luke twisted. He went down hard on his stomach, losing his breath. She slapped at his pack, each whack shoving him deeper into the dirt. He tried to suck air into his lungs. *Jesus, she's strong.* Her growl filled his ears, and her stink mingling with the bear spray gagged him. She tried to turn him over, but he pressed himself into the ground, grateful for the big pack that protected his neck. If the bear succeeded in flipping him, he'd have to fight. He felt for the tomahawk and this time, pulled the Velcro sheath apart.

The growling suddenly stopped, and Luke heard the bear gasp for air. *The spray must have taken hold.* He turned slightly and saw the sow shake her head, drool dripping from her mouth. She backed away and shuffled toward her cubs.

Luke lay still and listened, but heard only the bang of his heart against the ground. He rolled over to his side and listened again. Nothing. She and the cubs were gone.

He edged out of his pack and checked himself all over. He felt as though he'd been thrown under a bus, but he'd been lucky. The tender spot on his cheekbone would produce a good-sized bruise, but the bone wasn't broken. Other than that, he'd received only a few scratches. His pack was ripped in several places, but it was fixable.

Luke pulled out his first-aid kit. He cleaned the scratches with sterile wipes before smearing on antibiotic ointment and applying Band-Aids on the deeper ones.

The encounter had lasted only seconds, but it had seemed much longer. His legs felt shaky and his heart still beat rapidly. He took in deep breaths. He hadn't reacted as quickly as he should have, as quickly as he once did. Granddad wouldn't have been pleased.

The great-grandson of a Chippewa chief, Granddad had taken Luke under his wing when Luke was a young boy. While his older brothers played football and baseball, Luke spent much of his youth in the north woods of Wisconsin with Granddad. He'd learned to track and walk long distances, to make a fire, to hunt for a meal. If not always fun, Granddad's wilderness curriculum became a standard in Luke's life.

At 15, after Luke had taken down a rabbit with his tomahawk, Granddad had presented him with a bear claw in a Chippewa ceremony where youths became warriors. The claw symbolized courage. "For our Chippewa ancestors," he had said, "courage in the face of danger defines a man."

According to custom they had also prepared a feast. Granddad had shown him how to skin the rabbit, which he presented to his mother. His father and brothers attended the feast of rabbit stew, but afterward, Granddad had motioned for Luke to follow him outside.

"Let's go to the shed," he said.

"Why, Granddad?"

"That's where we conclude the ceremony. Bring your tomahawk."

Inside the shed, Granddad pressed tobacco into the bowl of the tomahawk then lit it. He inhaled and passed the tomahawk to Luke, who promptly gagged on the smoke. The door opened and closed. It was Luke's mother. She sat next to her son and took the pipe, drawing in deeply. Luke stared at his mother as she smoked. It wasn't often that she spoke of her heritage or engaged in any traditions. Before she left, she touched the bear claw hanging from Luke's neck and then touched his face.

Luke turned to his grandfather. "I'll never take it off, Granddad."

"Good. And now you will receive a totem of a hunter. For the Chippewa, there is no occupation more respected."

"Hunters and fishers," Granddad explained, "possess not only endurance and strength, skills in tracking and stalking, but also resourcefulness."

He placed his hands on Luke's shoulders. "You are Amik, the beaver."

⁂ ⁂ ⁂

LUKE HAD RESPECTED the totem chosen for him, but had nagged Granddad to teach him to fight, as a defender. He'd learned to handle knives, tomahawks, rocks, sticks, and his hands. Because of his grandfather, Luke had grown into a highly skilled and confident woodsman. He hunted as accurately with a tomahawk as with a bow and arrow. Using one had become innate.

But he had lost that intuition. He'd barely gotten the tomahawk's sheath undone in time. And it'd been the bear who had shown courage.

Luke fingered his neck, no longer ringed with the bear claw. At a college party he'd reluctantly taken it off to show it to some drunken student who'd then tossed it out the window. He never found it.

He picked up the Bear-Be-Gone. A can of spray had saved him. A can of spray. Luke hadn't wanted to bring it. With the Sierra's steep ascents and descents, he needed as light a pack as possible, but the spray had likely saved his life, or at least a limb or two.

"Thank you, Marina," he muttered. Marina was a school nurse and overly concerned with health and safety—he thought anyway. When he began sorting items for his trip, she'd gone through his first-aid kit 10 times, checking to see that it contained everything to take care of any emergency. When he refused to include the heavy utility knife with its nine blades, explaining the tomahawk would be enough, Marina had shrugged and left the room. It was a manner he'd found increasingly common in her. Removed. Cool. She seemed to forget he was pretty good at taking care of himself. Maybe offering unnecessary tools was her way of being a part of his journey. He didn't really know.

Luke replaced his first-aid kit and put on a long-sleeved shirt. Before he shouldered his pack, he patched the rips with duct tape. Thru-hikers were never without a few feet wrapped around their trekking poles for a quick repair.

In a couple of miles, the rhythm in Luke's legs returned and his heart steadied. In an hour, he was in a snowfield heading toward Forester Pass. He listened to the crunch of his boots as he kicked the toe of each one through the crust. Only faint prints from other hikers' boots showed on the snow's surface. No one had been here recently. To his left, the mountainside rose steeply and disappeared into the peaks. To his right, the snowfield dropped abruptly to the tree line. One bad step and he'd slide a thousand feet down the slope. But he welcomed the chance to focus on something as simple, and as crucial, as where he placed his feet.

At a slightly wider part of the trail, Luke stopped to catch his breath. The altimeter strapped to his wrist read 13,000 feet. Another few hundred and he'd be at the pass. It would be slow going. He'd started the hike in less-than-prime shape. Even running and swimming hadn't fended off the flab that had accumulated over the past years. A few months ago at the beach, his daughters had shouted "Jelly Belly!" at him in unison. He felt his sides. With a small sense of satisfaction, he noticed the flab, at least, had disappeared. He couldn't say as much for his strength, which he badly needed to survive the Sierras.

Luke closed his eyes and listened—other than the internal laboring of his heart and lungs, complete silence. He opened them. The sky was so clear and sharp, even the blue had an edge to it. This is what he had come for—to find a place where the only noise was his heartbeat, the only view that of unending sky, towering mountains, and deep valleys.

Six weeks ago, Marina had dropped him off at the trailhead near Campo, California, close to the Mexican border. "Happy retirement," she'd said, giving him a slight, stingy hug. The road followed the trail for half a mile, and Marina had driven slowly alongside, watching him take his first hundred steps. Then the road cut east and she was gone. Watching the dust kick up behind their four-by-four, Luke had felt both regretful and relieved.

Marina hadn't been happy he had retired from the FBI so young and then taken five months to hike the Pacific Crest Trail, leaving her to deal with their twin, teenaged daughters. He couldn't blame her there, but it was something he'd had to do. The girls had been excited for him, and although Marina had helped him pack and agreed to send re-supply boxes, she lapsed into polite conversation whenever he called from his cell phone. Twenty years ago, she would have reacted differently, been excited, like the kids. She used to love adventures.

"Come on," she'd said, when he was contemplating the move to the Los Angeles FBI office. "It'll be fun. We'll drive across the country, make all the important stops like the Grand Canyon."

After they had settled in Ventura County about an hour north of Los Angeles, it was Marina who suggested spontaneous motorcycle rides into the hills. It was Marina who planned midnight picnics to the beach. What had happened? Had the Bureau poisoned her as well?

Luke shifted his pack and readjusted the straps to decrease the weight pulling at his hips. He studied the trail ahead. It had taken him from the hot dust of Campo, through grasslands and canyons, through the dry mountains of Southern California, into the vast Mojave Desert, then up to the lush valleys of Kennedy Meadows, and now, into the High Sierras with their challenges of treacherous river crossings, steep ascents, and high altitudes—and some of the most beautiful views in the world. Since the southern end of the Sierras range, Luke hadn't crossed a road or seen a telephone line or vehicle. The smoggy, car-filled Los Angeles Basin he'd commuted through each day for 10 years seemed a lifetime away. Only the occasional contrail from a jet indicated that any kind of civilization existed.

Luke hoped his effort would bring deliverance. He had worked through blisters and sore muscles, long days of hiking and short nights of sleeping in a tent. Each night, feet elevated to relieve the swelling, meant another chance to eliminate the ghosts of his last years in the FBI and dampen the sting of the betrayal by an organization he had been so loyal to. His expertise had been counterterrorism and counterintelligence, and he had excelled in both areas. He'd found would-be bombers, tracked terrorists with spot-on surveillance, arrested a Soviet spy. He had kept America safe. But excellence was not rewarded. Instead, the system had plugged management vacancies with him, placed him wherever they needed a body who would work. On top of it, he'd been made a scapegoat during his last three years with the Bureau. The conversation with his supervisor hadn't yet left him. Every cell in his body retained it.

※　※　※

"Here's a copy of the inspector's report." Harry slid the report across the table. Luke flipped through it and stopped. He caught his breath and read more closely. "I was too loyal?"

He looked up at Harry. "So loyal to my agents that I was blinded to what was going on with TJ and failed to question him further? And that I lacked leadership?" Luke slammed the report on the table. "You've got to be fucking joking!"

His supervisor stared out the window, as if a rare bird had suddenly flown by. He turned back to Luke. "'Fraid not, Luke. This is what Wu found. You want to know more? Let's get him in here."

Harry picked up the phone. "Sally, send in Wu, please."

The door opened immediately, and Lee Wu, an agent Headquarters sent to L.A. to determine the cause for the Tom Jenks/Trina Kim case, walked in.

Luke glared at him. "You know it's entirely unfair to accuse me of poor leadership in this case. I had no way of stopping Tom from sleeping with Trina. That started way before I got here. This is bullshit, Wu."

Lee Wu's face was expressionless. "I wasn't sent here to be fair. Congress needed to find someone culpable. After all, Trina was an important Bureau source for our investigations into China. And she was sleeping with Jenks—her handler? Come on. It should have been caught. You were in charge of this case, no matter who had it previously." He pointed at the file lying on the table. "This happened on your watch. That simple."

"I get that part," replied Luke. "You should have just said so. Instead, you interviewed people associated with me until you found something, anything. Two agents out of three entire squads squeaked and turned loyalty and leadership into a sin. That's what I don't get, Wu."

Luke fought to stay calm. "You circled the wagons around those Washington idiots who should have been found at fault. Then you set me up as the fall guy. To silence the critics and the media and let Congress think they're actually doing something. You betrayed me and everything I stand for, everything I've done for the Bureau and the country."

Luke didn't wait for a reply. He stalked out of Harry's office, leaving his supervisor and Wu to consider each other.

"Luke's a good agent," said Harry.

"Yeah, well I didn't have a choice. The director was breathing down my neck," replied Wu, gathering up his papers.

*   *   *

LUKE WAS OFFERED a lateral move out of counterterrorism to admin, but he had refused. Counting pencils while he "rechromed" himself wasn't going to work for him. He'd retired from the Bureau early and angry. He was only 48-years-old.

Luke sucked water out of his camel pack. Marina had understood his anger and frustration and why he'd wanted to retire as soon as he was eligible. Even supported him. But her empathy stopped when he avoided talking about the next step in his life. In their life. After so many years living in suburbs, he didn't want to stay in or near a city. She did.

He continued kicking into the steep snowfield. As he ascended, the snow gave way to bare trail. The footing was easier, but the high altitude slowed his progress. His breaths grew short. The path tucked under a rock cornice that looked as though it intended to break off from the wall and plunge into the valley below. Luke inched his way along.

In another 200 feet, he reached a narrow cleft in a 1,000-foot rock wall. A wooden sign said: Forester Pass. 13,180 feet. Breathing heavily, he found a spot away from the wind. The famous pass was only a third of the way to the Canadian border, but fellow hikers joked that it was all downhill from here. Luke looked out at the world that stretched in snow-capped peaks as far as he could see. It was at once desolate and sublime. He hadn't felt this content for a very long time. At that moment, he knew only a death or serious injury in his family would tear him from this journey.

TWO

ERRI DENSMORE made her way to a desk in a corner of the bull pen, a modular grouping in a large open area where 30 other analysts worked. Seven A.M. Good. She'd have an hour before most of the others arrived, including Alan, whose desk backed to hers. It was tough to concentrate when for half the morning, he sneezed and cleared his sinuses. As analysts for the Counterterrorism Squad, she and the other members of the bull pen looked at information that came into the L.A. FBI office from domestic and foreign sources and hunted for trends, trying to connect the dots to any impending threat. The quiet of early morning allowed her to skip obligatory greetings and get right to work. She'd do all the talking she needed later on in the day when the analysts met to discuss threats.

Terri turned on the computer and typed in her password, then clicked open the secure email, scanning the long list of new messages. Most of them were requests relating to ongoing investigations—follow-up interviews, surveillance of subjects being investigated, reviews of security camera and

13

telephone records, outreach to authorities with vulnerable infrastructures such as a public utility grid.

Halfway down, several subject lines caught her eye. More messages from the new Terrorism Tracking Center in northern Virginia had accumulated overnight. The messages showed huge spikes in suspected terrorist activities. In Pakistan and Kashmir, terrorist groups were meeting more frequently. Cell phone usage in Indonesia, Malaysia, and Chechnya—countries known to harbor militant groups—had risen sharply. Terry leaned back in her chair. *These groups seem to be popping up everywhere. And they're talking a lot.*

The intel disturbed her. In the past few weeks, she'd also noted concurrent increases in activities of individuals and groups targeted for investigation in Southern California. Terri sensed patterns just under the surface. Patterns pointing to terrorism. The FBI and other anti-terrorist agencies aimed to stay ahead of these activities, and her job was an important part of revealing and sharing the leads. She decided to summarize this batch of new intel and send it upstairs to the counterterrorism squad—not that anyone up there would read and think about them. The squad's new supervisor, Dirk Barnstable, didn't exactly radiate confidence in his agents or in the analysts. He had served on a squad doing drug investigations in Detroit where he'd been known as an aggressive criminal agent, a real can-do sort of guy. Terri knew this was the kind of super G-man the public worshipped, the kind the FBI director wanted to head up counterterrorism after 9/11. But a lot of these agents only gave the appearance of chasing terrorists. In reality, many arrested anyone with a Muslim name for immigration violations or for selling knock-off videos. Whatever might ease the fear of another terrorist attack.

Terri looked at the calendar. It hadn't been the same since Luke left. He'd respected her knowledge and welcomed her opinions. He'd also been a handsome, if enigmatic man. Not until he was gone had Terri realized the small crush she'd had on him. She remembered asking Luke about the length of his hair—much longer than regulation—one morning while they waited together for the elevator. The question had popped out her mouth. He'd smiled slyly, those dark brown eyes concentrated into mock seriousness. "Rebellious, I guess," was all he'd said. Terri had blushed and mumbled something about it being daring. He'd gazed down at her with an amused look until she rushed off the elevator at the fifth floor.

A pang of guilt shot through her. Luke had been blamed for a mismanaged case that had happened years before he arrived at the L.A. office. They had all liked and respected Luke, but, make a wrong move in the Bureau, piss someone off, and down the toilet go your chances for advancement. Terri had only been at the L.A. office for a few months. At the time, she had felt too strongly about making a good start, and so, other than declaring Luke was a nice guy, she hadn't defended him. No one had, except Charlie Logan. He'd tried to set the record straight, stating bluntly that any case against Luke was bullshit. But his assertion hadn't mattered. Terri hadn't forgotten the look of anguish on Luke's face the day he told the analysts he'd be stepping down from his supervisory post.

It had turned out okay for Charlie, though. Despite standing by the doomed agent, he was now the FBI's program coordinator for the Joint Terrorism Task Force in L.A., one of 65 such forces formed after 9/11 to investigate threats and share intelligence with other national and local law enforcement agencies. It was a plum job, and Charlie was "mum" about Luke in the office. He'd probably been told to shut his mouth and "tow the line." But it didn't take coffeepot chit-chat to know Luke was missed there. Now and then she heard about his trip from Charlie, and the most recent update reported that Luke had reached the Sierras. Good for him. She hoped Luke was kicking butt out there.

Terri's thoughts returned to the messages. She wasn't sure Barnstable would realize the significance of the intel. Probably he didn't even know where India and Kashmir were. She considered bypassing him and contacting Charlie directly, but decided to follow protocol. Maybe Barnstable had gotten smarter these past few months. She began to write a threat summary of her conclusions to send up to him. He better act on this, she thought, typing quickly.

THREE

GENNADY ZUKOV took another pull at his cigarette and stubbed it out. It was between classes, and the coffee shop next to the campus had filled with students and professors. He eyed the cigarette butts piling up in the tin ashtray. Disgusting. He really had to quit. He drank his coffee and continued reading the engineering journal spread open on the table. He had another half hour before he taught his last class of the day and then he'd go on his nightly run. In his younger years, he'd been a good wrestler with a strong body, and despite smoking, he intended on keeping his middle-aged frame in shape.

A man slid into the empty chair on the other side of the table and placed a short stack of magazines near Gennady's journal. Gennady looked up. It was Maxsim Kovalenko, not only an old comrade from his days with the KGB, but his brother-in-law. Maxsim had stayed with the KGB after it was dismantled in 1991 and morphed into the Federal Security Service. He had joined the department that dealt with terrorism, with a focus on nuclear facilities.

17

"Maxsim. It's been a while," said Gennady, genuinely pleased to see his brother-in-law.

"Gennady," said Maxsim, avoiding a return greeting. "I don't have much time, and it was a great risk for me to come here, so please listen. And continue drinking your coffee."

Gennady was taken aback by Maxsim's abruptness. They had been roommates at university and helped each other through some of the toughest parts of training at the KGB. He had married Maxsim's sister, Vlada. Since Gennady had retired, they didn't see each other often. But still, there was no one he trusted more.

"I think someone is smuggling dirty stuff into the West, perhaps even the United States," Maxsim said.

Gennady did not change the expression on his face. He lit another cigarette. "What makes you think so?"

"I have good reason to believe a Russian general is stealing nuclear material from one of our storage areas. Security is lax at those places, and this general's been paying off the men in charge to look the other way. We're pretty sure he sells it to Chechnyan rebels."

Gennady didn't respond. He was aware that safety measures in many Russian nuclear facilities were weak, making them an easy source of dirty bomb material. He'd just read a newspaper article about nuclear thieves scavenging hospital equipment and lighthouse batteries for radioactive substances to sell.

He also knew that efforts to control smuggling of nuclear and radioactive material in foreign countries were poorly coordinated and badly administered, policies that resulted in foul-ups and in equipment left in packing crates, sometimes for years. On top of it, many sectors of the government remained corrupt, linked to organized crime. This was not the way Russia wanted to appear to the rest of the world.

Maxsim lowered his voice. "Last week, our security people raided a terrorist camp in Chechnya and found plans for taking nuclear material into Pakistan. The rebels have ties to many militant groups beyond the Taliban. We're looking at groups in Uzbekistan and Kyrgyzstan. You know the United States runs anti-terrorist training bases in those countries. We don't like them there, but the militants like it less. All of them hate the West. It's logical to assume that they may target the United States and other Western countries."

Maxsim leaned toward Gennady. "We tried to arrest this general, but his brother is a high-ranking politician. You know how that goes."

Gennady considered his brother-in-law for a moment. "Why tell me? I'm just an engineering professor. Terrorism wasn't my specialty at the KGB."

Maxsim smiled for the first time since he'd sat down. "The heavyweights are out of control here, Gennady, and our government is too corrupt to handle it. I believe you stay in touch with a special friend in America. Maybe he can help."

Maxsim stood up. "This is bad business, Gennady. Contact him—for Russia."

He picked up the magazines, all but one. "You might find the article on page 67 of some interest." The FSB agent slipped behind a couple of students leaving the coffee shop.

Gennady finished his coffee. He tucked the magazine inside his engineering journal and headed back to the campus. It started to drizzle. Just what Moscow needed to start the summer—more rain. He hadn't thought about Luke Chamberlin for a long time. In the 1990s, they'd been on opposite sides of the fence. He'd been a KGB agent working undercover as a scientist at the Soviet Mission to the United Nations in New York. He allegedly studied water quality and irrigation in developing countries. But his real intention had been to find a source of technical information, a knowledgeable person who would sell secrets.

Luke had been the persistent agent who'd followed him all over the New York boroughs and then caught him taking classified documents in a sting operation. He hadn't expected Luke to do his job so well. The FBI agent had been observant and relentless. He seemed to have a sixth sense that placed him always in his path. The KGB operatives nicknamed him *vernyi pyos* –faithful hound. "*Vernyi pyos*," Gennady repeated. He thought back to the aftermath of his capture.

"It's quite a circus," Luke had said while leading Gennady handcuffed through the parade of media gathered outside the Federal Building for the obligatory "perp walk." Gennady had been surprised at the FBI agent's honesty but only nodded with a small smile of acknowledgment. Nor had he answered any questions during his interrogation.

But in the weeks prior to his deportation, an unusual friendship developed between the two agents. They discussed patriotism, a sense of duty to their countries, and a work ethic rarely found in each other's services. They had talked about their mutual love of hiking in mountains, their summer homes, and how much they enjoyed respites there.

Gennady turned his collar up against the rain and walked up the wide granite steps to the Engineering Building at Moscow State University. Although from a small working-class town, he had easily passed the testing to be an engineer. He had dreamed of building bridges. At the university, he met Vlada and then Maxsim. His dreams changed. Vlada's father was career KGB and recognized in Gennady the talent to be an agent—friendly, good with people, bright, and with a taste for travel. Above all, Gennady loved his country. Vlada had pressured him to join the KGB. Being the wife of a KGB agent or a foreign service officer was one of the very few ways a woman could travel outside the Soviet Union at that time, and she had wanted to see the world.

Gennady had agreed, and they found themselves first in Geneva, then South Africa, and finally in New York City. His expertise had been finding and co-opting civilian scientists and engineers who, after years of vetting by the KGB, would be in a position to obtain secrets. The targets were often third world émigrés or students who might feel sympathetic to Soviet ideals. Gennady had felt fairly secure in spying. He had found an easy target, an engineering student from Ecuador, and had been adept at handling him. With little convincing, the poor student had been willing to give him technical material in exchange for money. Looking back, he had gotten caught up in the thrill, the power. He never should have taken such a risk with only limited diplomatic immunity. He'd grown over-confident and careless. The FBI caught him.

It had happened at a subway stop in Brooklyn where he had planned to meet the student. At the agreed-upon time, he hadn't noticed anything unusual, just a couple embracing nearby. Just as he accepted the documents from the student, the couple drew apart and approached him.

"FBI," they had simply said, holding up their badges. "You're under arrest for espionage."

They'd handcuffed him and spoken briefly to the student who walked away.

Luke had been waiting in a car outside.

Beyond his respect for Luke, the Soviet spy owed him— and the United States. After pleading *nolo contendere*, Gennady was sentenced to stay out of America for five years. The U.S. and Soviet Union were undergoing important negotiations and didn't want the media focused on the case, so it was kept quiet. The collapse of the Soviet Union soon followed. During that time, Gennady's daughter, Veronika, grew ill.

When leukemia was finally diagnosed, he and his family were able to travel back to the States for medical help. Luke had pulled strings to have Veronika treated at a children's hospital in Los Angeles. The little girl had died, but Gennady was grateful to the doctors and nurses who'd tried so hard to save her. He was especially grateful to Luke. Between long stays in the waiting room and breaks at the Chamberlin's home, the families had grown close. No doubt Maxsim knew all of this.

Gennady closed the door to his small office. It wasn't much bigger than a closet and had no window, but he didn't share it with another professor. He opened the magazine to page 67. Printed on the page was a tiny stamp. Gennady's heart beat faster. He knew the stamp was filled with microscopic text. He pulled open a drawer and rummaged around in it. He opened another, pawing through papers until he spotted what he'd been looking for—a lens. He found his old microscope in the back of a cupboard and affixed the lens to it, then placed the stamp underneath and looked through the eye piece. In a few minutes he learned further details of the FSB raid in Chechnya and the likely route of the dirty material as far as Pakistan. He memorized the information, then ran the magazine through a shredder.

He checked his watch and hurried down the hallway to his classroom. Maxsim was right. This was bad business. He felt weighted down by the information, yet somehow excited. Was it the thrill in being in the game again? Doing something other than teaching basic engineering? Helping his beloved Russia once more?

It had been a couple of years since he had spoken to Luke. Gennady wondered if he still had his home phone number.

FOUR

L UKE MADE HIS WAY along the trail that led to Muir
Pass. Glacier-scoured Sierras rose like jagged spires. A
sanctuary of dark, dense lakes and flower-flushed meadows surrounded him, and he stopped for a moment to let his
senses absorb their beauty.

This part of the PCT was named after the famous natu-
ralist who had spent weeks at a time hiking the area in the
late 1800s. Luke had devoured John Muir's seminal book, *My
First Summer in the Sierra*, but he hadn't truly understood the
book's passages until now, when Muir's words about the High
Sierras penetrated: "Surely the brightest and best of all the
Lord has built." He couldn't agree more—and today, he had
all of it to himself. Today, he felt some of the past lift from
his shoulders, some of the dissatisfaction and sense of failure
wash away in a rushing alpine stream. In the peaks ahead, he
saw possibility. He felt it in his legs.

Luke began an ascent up a canyon, toward Muir Pass, walking between polished granite walls streaked with tumbling
waterfalls. He felt the pressure of the gear on his back and

recollected from his readings that Muir had carried only a wool overcoat, tea, and a loaf of bread to last him days. *What's happened to people*, he mused. *We're so reliant on technology, we can hardly find our way out of our own houses without GPS.* Between email, video conferencing, BlackBerries, iPhones, and the like, he'd had enough of being plugged in. He carried an altimeter, which also was a compass and watch, and a cell phone for emergencies and to stay in touch with his family, but had opted not to carry GPS. Granddad and the Marine Corps had supplied all the survival skills he needed—plus a few drugs Marina had tucked into his emergency packet.

The ascent was long and rocky, with 10 miles of it above tree line. He was heartened to feel power coming back to his legs and hoped his body would survive another 1,900 miles to the Canadian border. At this point, he had nearly completed the arduous passes. Three more after Muir, all of them easier than the first six, remained before he left the High Sierras. At the moment, he was on schedule and at this rate, would complete the hike before any early snowfalls stopped him farther north in Washington's Cascade Range.

Ahead came the unmistakable roar of a river running at high speed. In the Sierras, cold alpine nights lessened the flow of snowmelt-fed streams, offering hikers easier fords in the mornings. But it was already past 10 in the morning and Luke saw that the creek, though shallow, was moving fast. Even ankle-deep water, at this speed, was enough to unbalance and push over a big man. He'd been gangly and uncoordinated as a kid, and despite an accumulation of outback talents, he'd never achieved good balance. His height, plus a heavy pack, didn't help his stability. He didn't like fording water. A few wet-looking rocks poked above the swirls—a nightmarish crossing at best. He scanned them for a possible crossing pattern and using his trekking poles for balance, stepped onto the first rock. It held. Digging his poles into the creek bed, he stretched and reached for the second, then the third. It took only a slight wobble of the next rock for Luke to lose his balance. The weight of his body and pack brought him crashing onto the far bank. He lay for a moment in the dirt, his arms and trekking poles splayed, one foot still in the water. Gravel ground into his face. He dragged himself up to a sitting position and glanced around, grateful no other hikers had been there to witness the show. He rubbed his cheek and stood. *Twenty feet of snow won't stop me,* he thought getting back on the trail, *it's these lousy little creeks.*

At the tree line, Luke stopped to take a drink from his camel pack. Dehydration came quickly so high, followed often by a splitting headache. He noticed boot prints of other hikers though they were hard to see on the bare ground. Some were faded, barely visible, but others were fresher, perhaps a day or a few hours old. One set of boot prints wasn't spaced evenly, as if the hiker were having trouble staying balanced. Luke knew when someone wasn't moving smoothly. It looked like the hiker was stumbling. He was sure about this.

He'd spent time with the Shadow Wolves, a tactical patrol unit with the Immigration and Customs Enforcement Agency mostly made up of Native Americans. Shadow Wolf officers found smugglers who tried to cross the U.S.-Mexican border. Their esteemed history of tracking was passed down from generation to generation and based on traditional methods of tracking called "cutting for sign." A sign included any kind of physical evidence such as footprints, tire tracks, even thread. "Cutting" was searching for a sign.

With Granddad's lessons on tracking animals, it hadn't taken Luke long to master the Wolves' art. He'd learned to spot small items snagged on branches, even a single fiber of cloth, determine when a footprint was made, how large the person was, and whether he or she carried additional weight, even whether or not a horse carried a rider.

It was an experience that, beyond teaching him to cut sign, also had deepened Luke's native roots, that part of him that held the Chippewa sensibility and spirit. His time with the Shadow Wolves had helped define him as a man.

More than once he'd been called out of his jurisdiction to solve cases involving kidnapping, like the case in Georgia a few years ago, when a serial killer had kidnapped his young son and fled into the woods.

*   *   *

"I'm on my way," Luke said, hanging up the phone. He called Marina to let her know he was leaving right from the office to catch a plane from LAX to Atlanta. During the flight, he studied the report on the fugitive and kidnapper. The guy sounded like a crazed survivalist, a war vet with PTSD, the report said.

At Atlanta, he met up with the search team, Atlanta FBI, SWAT, members of the Georgia Bureau of Investigation, and FBI profilers from Quantico.

"Glad to have you," said the team leader, shaking Luke's hand. "It's a long way to the Chattahoochee National Forest. You can sleep in the van."

At the base of Springer Mountain, the location where they'd last looked, they unloaded guns and search equipment. They were well equipped, Luke noticed, with night vision goggles, flares, GPS, maps, radios, and even portable repeater towers. "We think he went up this way," one of the searchers pointed toward a densely forested, hilly area. "We followed tracks part way, then lost him. It's pretty thick up there."

Luke nodded, and they walked a couple of miles to where the search team had lost the fugitive's tracks. Luke looked around. The trees grew close together, and the undergrowth was thick. He listened for birds or squirrels that might be alarmed farther away. He squatted on the ground and felt for indentations and looked for leaves that had been kicked in one direction. He found the father's trail.

"That way," he said to the team. In another quarter mile, he stopped.

"The trail splits here. The fugitive must have known he was being followed. His son would have slowed him down. He likely left the boy here and continued alone."

"What an asshole," said a team member.

"He must have been desperate," replied Luke. "Hear that noise? It's a stream. A guy like him would know to follow it downhill. But he's probably not in any hurry to leave the woods. It won't take much for you to cut him off."

Luke turned away from the team. "I'll find the boy."

While the rest of the team returned the way they'd come, Luke carefully studied the boy's trail sign. His sneaker prints, broken branches, which way he'd kicked leaves, where he'd stepped on moss-covered rocks. For a couple of hours, the sign took Luke in frustrating circles and aimless patterns. Then the boy's trail veered off toward a stand of hemlock. Luke found him curled in a ball under low-lying hemlock branches, cold but alive. Luke opened his vest and shirt and tucked the boy to his chest.

*   *   *

LUKE TOOK A LAST GULP of water and resumed his ascent. His instincts for finding people hadn't translated to understanding them, especially women. He'd grown up in a house with a father, two brothers, and a quiet, hard-working mother. She'd never complained about anything, not even the toilet seat being left up. Now he wished she had. Marina and the twins never let him off the hook about the toilet seat. Such a small, harmless habit, too. What was the big deal about a toilet seat. To this day he didn't understand, and there sure hadn't been any GPS guiding him through marriage and parenthood. Granddad hadn't helped there either. His penchant for spending weeks at a time in the woods had shortened his one marriage to a couple of years.

Luke heard voices ahead and came to a small group of hikers gathered at the side of the trail. He nodded hello. They were a typical "unit" of thru-hikers: a strong, tattooed female surrounded by several males. Luke had heard of such units forming around a single female—until she tired of them and shooed them away. Another unit would form around her later. Probably it would be like this all the way to Canada.

"Looks like the lake's not much farther," Luke said.

"No, guess not," replied one of the male hikers.

They looked bushed.

Luke smiled. "See you up there."

At Helen Lake, the first of two desolate lakes named for Muir's daughters, Luke stopped to drink more water and chew on jerky. Again, he noticed faint boot prints in the gravel. They led to a group of rocks, and on a hunch, Luke followed them. Crouched against a boulder was a young hiker, not much older than his daughters. His knees were drawn up to his chest, and he seemed to be dozing with his head resting in his arms, his hat pulled over his face.

"You okay?" asked Luke. He touched the hiker's shoulder.

The young hiker looked up. His face was thin and drawn. A faint beard stubbled his chin. "Oh yeah," he replied. "Just needed a rest."

He peered at Luke, hesitating. "Got any extra water? Some food? I'm out."

Luke saw that the young man shivered in his T-shirt. Next to him was a small pack. Very small. This kid was an ultra-light hiker, and the wobbly boot prints were his. Ultra-light hikers traveled with the least amount of food and equipment they could. To save weight, they cut their toothbrushes in half, and used their clothes and gear for multiple purposes. Earlier on the trail Luke had heard a joke about them—that they eliminated carrying the weight of eye glasses by having laser surgery before they set out. The balance of not carrying as much pack weight was supposed to reduce the extra weight of water since there wouldn't be as much fluid loss. But the theory didn't always work. Case in point sitting right in front of him. Clearly, this ultra-lighter was exhausted and dehydrated. Without the extra weight of a water filtration system, he'd probably also picked up giardia from drinking contaminated water. The intestinal infection could take hikers off the trail for good.

Luke took off his pack and pulled out a water bottle. He wasn't happy about this and looked sharply at the hiker.

"What's your name?" He offered the water.

"Lightfoot." He gulped the water. "Thanks."

Luke rolled his eyes at the trail name. PCT hikers adopted a strange assortment of names while hiking. A whole culture grew around names like Eagle Eye, Sidewinder, Dirt Devil, Meadow Lark, Disco, and Happy Feet. Ritchie Rich had robbed banks and escaped along the PCT. He wasn't caught until he finished the trail and tried to rob a bank in Canada. Luke wondered if some ever reverted back to their real names once they left the trail. Right now this boy's feet didn't look so light.

"Not too fast," he said. Probably Lightfoot hadn't had any water for 10 miles. "Don't you know how easy it is to get dehydrated up here?" The question came out more gruffly than he intended.

"Yeah, I know. It's just that I was aiming to make Vermillion Ranch in three days. I didn't want to carry much. "

Luke knew he should wait with this idiot and make sure he was fit to travel again. But he didn't have time. He had a schedule to keep. Wasn't he done saving people? He stood up.

"Here's something to eat," he said, tossing Lightfoot a Snickers bar and a couple of packs of jerky. "You need to rest more. Then consider walking a ways with a group of hikers just coming up, until you feel better. There are a couple of streams ahead. Make sure you drink. After the water's been filtered."

"Wow. Thanks, man," said the hiker, tearing open the candy wrapper. "I'll do that."

Luke shouldered his pack. The encounter with Lightfoot had slowed his progress so that he had to deal with the softened snow of the afternoon. He soon found himself slogging through deep slabs of snow. He focused on kicking in a step with the toe of his boot, checking his balance, taking the step, then repeating the motion with the other boot. Once in a while, he stepped into snow up to his thigh.

The only sign of the trail was a narrow line of boot prints crisscrossing in long switchbacks up to the pass. The prints were large and fairly fresh. Another hiker, male, maybe a half mile ahead. Moving in a steady pattern. A good hiker. He'd follow them.

Luke finally reached the stone hut that honored John Muir and welcomed hikers to the pass. He leaned against the side of the building, exhausted.

Clouds were beginning to gather. Just a few wisps of high cirrus, but they were moving fast and looked like they might gather into clumps of cumulus.

"Hey," a voice called. Luke turned to find another man sitting nearby. He was short, strong muscular legs bare under hiking shorts. His graying beard surrounded an intense smile. A Navy wool watch cap covered his head.

"I'm Mike, Mike Cortez, also known as 'Sea Dog,'" he said, sticking out his hand. "Good climb?"

This time, Luke smiled at the trail name.

"Tough," he replied, returning Mike's handshake. "I'm Luke Chamberlin, or 'Camper'—something about my huge pack. I guess people think I like to camp."

"It's one of the biggest I've seen on the trail," said Mike. "What kind is it?"

"An old one," replied Luke, removing the pack from his back and setting it on the ground. "A Kelty external frame."

He opened the top flap to dig out lunch. "I've got 5,500 cubic inches of space in here—but it weighs nearly six pounds."

"Wouldn't surprise me if someone tried to climb in as a stowaway," Mike said, stifling a chuckle.

The temperature was falling fast, and the wind picked up. They ducked into the hut, which wasn't the least bit warm but offered shelter from the wind.

Luke noticed Mike's Navy knit cap. "You in the service?"

"Was," replied Mike, "SEALs. Senior Chief Mike Cortez at your service. Retired a couple of years ago."

"I was Marine Corps, then FBI," said Luke. "Just retired four months ago."

Mike laughed. "A jarhead. Wouldn't you know I'd meet one crawling around up here."

He glanced at Luke's belt. "And one with a hawk no less."

"It's as good as a knife," Luke said. "But I guess you'd know that."

He chewed on a piece of jerky. "What's a squid doing out of water?"

"I'm hiking the trail to raise money for families of soldiers killed overseas," Mike said. "I saw too many families left with nothing. Government doesn't come through for them."

Luke nodded. "I'm not surprised. I'm not hiking it for anything quite so altruistic. I've always wanted to hike the PCT since I read about it in a *National Geographic* as a kid."

Mike peered out of the hut. "Clouds are coming in, and they don't look friendly." He stood up. "We'd better get going. Are you up for some company?"

Although Luke liked the solace of hiking alone and the freedom to go at his own pace, he thought he'd enjoy walking with Mike for a while. "Sure," he replied, looking at his map. "Let's try to make it to Evolution Lake. We might find a decent place to camp there."

The two shrugged on their packs and picked their way along the trail, which turned down hill through more snowfields.

Luke found that Mike kept a pace about the same as his. But when lightning shot out of dark clouds, Mike increased his speed, and Luke struggled to keep pace with the more compact SEAL.

In a couple of miles, they reached the safety of the tree line. In another couple they arrived at Evolution Lake and found a good campsite among clumps of stunted white bark pines.

For the first time in a while, Luke found himself talking nonstop. Over re-hydrated, freeze-dried meals and hot tea, they reminisced about the military and discussed the government, politics, and hiking. *This guy rotates on the same planet as I do*, Luke thought.

This became even clearer when they touched on marriage, something Luke hadn't expected to open up about, particularly to a SEAL. "Twenty years and twin teens," Luke said. "It's mostly been a good time—when I've been home."

"My marriage didn't last once I became a SEAL," said Mike. "I was gone too much. Physically and emotionally," he explained. "No kids, thankfully. I haven't found another lady yet, but I know it takes more than returning from a mission a hero."

Rolled in his sleeping bag later that evening, Luke thought about Mike's admission that he'd missed too much while he was gone. Had he done the same? Had he missed so much that Marina had grown independent from him? Didn't need him anymore? Marina had always managed things so smoothly, he hadn't noticed what he was or wasn't doing as a parent. He suddenly felt on uneven ground with his wife, and his sleep was restless.

Luke and Mike hiked together another day, enjoying an easy camaraderie. When they reached a juncture where a secondary trail veered to Muir Ranch, Mike stopped. "I'm getting off here," he said. "Going to Florence Lake to re-supply and send emails to my sponsors." He handed Luke a scrap of paper. "This is my cell phone number." He didn't wait for Luke to give him his. "Catch you later."

They shook hands, and Mike turned toward Muir Ranch.

Luke zipped the number into a side pocket of his pack, somehow glad to have it.

He began his ascent to Selden Pass.

FIVE

MEDHI ASHRAD opened the door to his single-story brick home in a quiet neighborhood of Quetta. Although it was a hot summer evening, he lit the stove to boil water for tea. His hands were stiff from weaving carpets, and he rubbed his fingers while he waited for the water to heat. Medhi's father and grandfather had both been carpet makers, and, despite sore hands, Medhi was proud to carry on the tradition. Medallions and paisley motifs were his trademark. He had woven these exquisite patterns into his own prayer rug and those of his family.

Medhi lived alone. His wife had died from cancer less than a year ago, and both his daughters were married and lived in villages outside Quetta. Medhi's only son, Aban, was dead now, too. Just three months ago, he'd been playing with the son of a friend, a teacher at a religious school in the Pashtunabad neighborhood. Medhi knew his friend supported the Taliban, as many people in Quetta did. The Taliban had brought a measure of order to the people in this frontier border city.

What Medhi didn't know was that Quetta had become an important base for the Taliban, with its commanders holed

35

up in homes among Pashtunabad's narrow streets and tall mud walls. The Pakistani government insisted few Taliban members were there, and Medhi had believed Aban was safe.

∗   ∗   ∗

"You get the ball," said Hamid to Aban outside his home in Pashtunabad on a warm May afternoon. The ball they'd been kicking back and forth rolled into the street.

"No, you get it," laughed Aban. "You kicked it there."

While the two boys argued about the soccer ball, a U.S.-made, pilotless drone flew over Quetta. Controlled by people thousands of miles away in the Nevada desert, the robotic aircraft slowed over Pashtunabad to less than 100 miles per hour.

Hamid retrieved the ball from the street.

The drone hovered near his house.

"You'll have to get it the next time." He kicked the ball to Aban.

Not far from Las Vegas a desk-top warrior pressed a button. The drone's supersonic Hellfire missile launched with barely a whisper. Its precise targeting system shot it through a window into Hamid's house, aiming for a powerful Taliban leader. But only low-level members and teachers had congregated inside.

∗   ∗   ∗

FOR THE SECOND TIME IN A YEAR, Medhi's relatives and neighbors came together to mourn a family member. For the second time, they gathered in a common courtyard for funeral prayers and then took what was left of Aban to the family gravesite to lie next to his mother.

Medhi's loss pressed on all parts of him like a heavy, dark fog. He couldn't dispose of the colorful tablecloth his wife had sewn. He couldn't enter his son's room. If it hadn't been for his pigeons, Medhi didn't know how he'd have gotten through his grief. The pigeons, his hatred for Americans, and his secret work for Islam kept him going.

After his son's death, Medhi was told that the Pakistani government's intelligence about the house had been vague. They had thought a Taliban leader was moving arms, fighters, and money into southern Afghanistan from the house. But Medhi had learned the more likely truth—that in a secret arrangement, the United States and Pakistani governments had permitted more and more deadly strikes with drones—with, or without, good intelligence. The Pakistani government didn't want its people to know it was supporting the United States, so warnings of impending strikes were not issued. Aban had simply been collateral damage. It happened all over Pakistan.

It had taken little encouragement for Medhi to decide to help the Taliban. Up until Aban's death, Medhi had been a moderate Sunni Muslim, like most of Pakistan's population. He had believed in the basic tenets of Islamic Law—generosity, fairness, daily prayer, almsgiving, observance of Ramadan, a pilgrimage to Mecca. He hadn't believed in the extreme practices of Taliban militants—the tyranny and terrorism they created.

Aban's death changed all of that. The struggle to rid his society of a corrupt government and foreign oppression was now Medhi's. He had joined the jihad. And so had his birds.

The sound of cooing from the roof brought a small smile to Medhi's face. He climbed the outside stairs that led to the rooftop loft. Thirty sleek homing pigeons, of different colors and patterns, crowded around the door, anxious for their daily flight. He'd kept homing pigeons since he was a boy, learning from his father to raise and race them. Although racing the birds could be traced back to the Mughal era when only kings and the rich kept pigeons, anybody could raise and race them now. They were easy and cheap to breed, so even the poorest could afford them. There were several racing clubs in the city, and sometimes Medhi managed to win a bit of money in local events. While he could never afford to travel to international races in the U.A.E., Dubai, Qatar, or Bahrain, he'd make it to Lahore later this year. The Pakistan Pigeon Club hosted an annual race there, and winners went home with cash, and sometimes a car.

Before Medhi released the birds, he counted them and found 31. He clapped his hands. *Good. Hassan has returned.* He entered the small loft and picked up the tired pigeon that had settled close to his mate.

Medhi held Hassan gently. He stroked the glossy grey feathers. "You are fast, Hassan. You will do well at the race in Lahore, for sure. But first, you will fly for our cause, for Allah. Already, you are a hero."

Medhi rubbed his cheek against Hassan's smooth back and kissed the pigeon on the top of his head. He couldn't help but think the spirits of his wife and son soared in the bird's wings, and would guide Hassan and all of his birds to success.

From Hassan's leg, Medhi took a small aluminum capsule. Then he returned the tired bird to the loft and opened the door for the rest of the pigeons to fly. For a moment, Medhi watched. In a group, the flock dipped and swerved, and then disappeared over the rooftops, heading for the hills that surrounded Quetta. *How lucky you are to fly far from the ruins of our country.*

Medhi took the aluminum capsule back downstairs. He poured a cup of tea and sat at the kitchen table. Carefully, he twisted the capsule open and removed the tiny roll of thin paper. On it were a few lines of Urdu, jumbled in a code.

Medhi had memorized the decoding process and in a minute, he knew what the simple message said. *Send your contact to the port. Rug arriving on the third.* Medhi glanced at his calendar. The third was next week. The pigeon post had worked perfectly. For several weeks, pigeons flying along a string of lofts had been carrying messages throughout terrorist cells that stretched from Chechnya, through Uzbekistan, and into Pakistan. Hassan had waited his turn in the last loft in the northwestern part of Pakistan where Taliban strongholds protected militant groups. American spyware, designed to trace phone calls and listen to people's conversations, had been too advanced to catch a seemingly common pigeon. Hassan had flown the 200 miles without incident.

Now, Medhi would send a human messenger via bus to Karachi to deliver a message to a rug seller there. In his note, Medhi would describe a new style of carpet he was designing, but the words would speak a different truth. The rug seller would set in motion the next step in Allah's name.

Medhi had an hour before evening prayers. He burned the message and climbed back to the rooftop carrying his tea and peanuts for Hassan. He relaxed in a folding chair. A breeze cooled his skin under the cotton salwar kameez. He slowly drank the tea, awaiting the return of his marvelous birds.

He looked at the darkening sky. *It will be clear tonight. I will see many stars.*

SIX

BY MOSCOW STANDARDS, the Sparrow Hills three-bedroom apartment Gennady shared with Vlada and their son, Sasha, was large. The apartment building abutted a park and their place overlooked the Moscow River and city beyond. The third bedroom served as Gennady's office. It was crammed with engineering textbooks, political tomes about the Cold War, and Russian and English novels.

Gennady glanced at the student papers piled high on his desk. He'd get to them later.

"I'm leaving," called Vlada from the living room. "You alright?"

Gennady had been quiet at dinner. He hadn't asked Sasha about school. Nor had he made the usual fuss about the meal. Vlada knew she wasn't a very good cook, but she appreciated Gennady's nightly praise of whatever she made.

"Yes, fine. Just tired," he replied. "I've got a pile of papers to correct tonight."

Gennady made a point of walking from his office into the living room. "Enjoy the movie," he said. "What are you seeing?"

"Oh, that new Borak comedy," replied Vlada. "I'm going with Lara, so we'll probably have coffee afterward."

"I'll be asleep by the time you're back," said Gennady and kissed his wife on the cheek.

With Vlada at a movie and Sasha at a friend's for the evening, he'd have time alone. It was 7 P.M. He did a quick calculation in his head. It would be 6 A.M. in California. Maybe Luke hadn't left for work yet.

Gennady returned to his office and searched the bookshelf until he saw the book he wanted. He pulled the engineering textbook from the bookcase and opened it to a page about two thirds of the way through. Folded in half and tucked into the crease were several thin pieces of paper covered in names and contact information set in small type.

He put on his glasses and scanned the list that contained people from his covert past—names of officials at the UN Secretariat, social contacts, people he'd approached to work "assignments" for him, co-optees, and other spies. Some were still written in code. He came to Luke Chamberlin, *vernyi pyos*.

Gennady picked up the go-phone he'd bought on his way home from the university. Although he was retired, he was sure his calls were periodically traced. He didn't want to leave any kind of a trail leading to this particular conversation. He held the phone in his hand. He thought back to Luke's dogged tailing of his family in and out of New York's boroughs, Marina holding Vlada's hand at the hospital day after day, their vacation in Switzerland, later, when the families hiked in the Alps together, the twins making Sasha laugh again. He took a deep breath and punched in the international code for the United States, then Luke and Marina's home phone number.

He tightened his grip on the phone. *What would Luke say? How would he react to what sounded like a far-out movie plot?*

"Hello?" answered Marina.

"Marina, it's Gennady Zukov. I know I'm calling early."

"Gennady? It's wonderful to hear from you. At any hour." Marina replied.

She fired a number of questions at him. How was Vlada? Did Sasha still play tennis? Was he still teaching? Gennady was fluent in English, but he replied slowly and carefully. Yes, his family was fine, teaching was going well.

"Is Luke home?" he asked.

"Luke retired, Gennady," said Marina. "He's hiking the Pacific Crest Trail. You know, the trail that runs from Mexico to Canada."

"Oh, yes, he used to talk about that." Gennady had wanted to hike in the Adirondacks when he was stationed in New York, but he hadn't been able to travel beyond a 50-mile radius from the United Nations—a reciprocation from the U.S. government for the restrictions placed on American diplomats stationed in Moscow at the time. He had never walked much past Central Park.

"I'm glad he finally went," said Gennady. "How long will he be gone?"

"Oh, if he stays on schedule, it'll take him five months."

"That's quite a hike. I'm jealous."

"Is there a particular reason you called, Gennady?" asked Marina. "Can I get a message to him for you?"

"I was just thinking of him," replied Gennady quickly. "We haven't spoken for a long while, and I wondered if he still felt frustrated with his job."

"You can say that again," said Marina. "He retired from the Bureau the first day he was eligible. He couldn't wait to get out. Problem is, he doesn't have anything planned, and we've got two kids to get through college. There are lots of good jobs in security for former FBI agents, but Luke wants none of them. And I can't send two children through college on a part-time school nurse's salary."

Gennady heard the irritation in Marina's voice. He changed the subject. "Where along the trail is he now?"

"He just called from the Sonora Pass in California."

"Sounds high," Gennady continued, hoping he sounded casual. "Where is that?"

"Oh, Sonora Pass is just east of San Francisco," answered Marina. "He'll be at Lake Tahoe in a couple of days."

"Oh yes, I've heard of Lake Tahoe. Will you see him?"

"No, I've got too much going on with the kids."

Again, Gennady heard tension in Marina's voice. "Well, tell him I say hello and good luck. Next time I call, it will be to say congratulations."

"I will, Gennady. Give my love to Vlada and come visit soon."

Gennady hung up the phone. *So Luke is hiking the Pacific Crest Trail. What pushed him to actually do the entire thing? Leave his family for half a year and put his future on hold. Sounds like more than a childhood dream.*

He carefully replaced Luke's number in the engineering book. *Luke must have gotten kicked around by the system.* Gennady had had the same sense of betrayal after he'd been arrested and expelled from the U.S. He'd become *persona non grata* to most of his peers, not only at the Soviet Mission in New York, but in Moscow where he'd been summarily discharged from the KGB without so much as a thanks. Even his connection to Vlada's father, who had passed away just before his deportation, hadn't made things easier.

But he'd gotten over it and Vlada hadn't been as angry as he'd thought. They had gone on with their lives, even with the tragedy of losing Veronika. He and Luke had similar values and shared similar experiences, but it sounded like Luke was having a harder time letting go of the bad times.

Gennady found a beer in the refrigerator and turned back to his desk. With Luke in the middle of nowhere and no longer connected to the Bureau, contacting him was going to be harder than he thought. What had Marina said? Luke wasn't far from San Francisco. He poured the beer into a glass. He used to know someone who worked out of there. That agent was retired though, with little way of reaching him. Then he thought of his brother-in-law. Maxsim was the one person he knew who could contact an agent at the Russian consulate in San Francisco.

Gennady looked at the calendar. Wednesday. The weekend was coming up. They hadn't seen Maxsim and his family for a couple of months, and now that the weather had warmed, a Sunday picnic might be just the thing. He picked up the phone. Feelings he'd forgotten—excitement, trepidation, fear—rushed back. He hesitated, then punched in Maxsim's number.

In a few minutes, Gennady hung up. The picnic was arranged. He and Maxsim would go on a walk. They would talk. About sports, their families—other things. Gennady looked around for his pack of cigarettes. He was about to step way out of bounds to get a message to Luke, one he knew the ex-FBI agent wouldn't want to hear, or believe. The last thing Gennady wanted to do was pull Luke off the trail and keep him from finishing something he had so looked forward to doing—let alone put him in danger. Gennady knew Luke had never been afraid of anything, but nor did he look for trouble. Gennady sighed. *Well, Luke, old friend, I just may have brought trouble to you.*

He lit a cigarette and turned to the stack of student papers.

SEVEN

THE WHEELS of the reyri hit a rock, lifting Mahmoud Bakr off his seat. He grabbed the side of the wooden cart with one hand and with the other, reached to hold his skull cap on. The driver muttered and flapped the reins at the donkey pulling the cart, as if the tired animal might consider altering its speed or course over the rutted mountain road. Mahmoud sat among a pile of fruits and woven blankets that were on their way to Batkhela to be sold at the bazaar. He felt lucky to have found a ride that far. Even a bone-jarring one was better than walking.

The Koran, a bottle of water, and a bit of bread and cheese crowded one side of the satchel Mahmoud carried. Rupees filled the other side. In his entire life, Mahmoud had never seen so much money; it underscored the importance of the mission he had accepted.

A few days ago, one of his teachers at the madrassa he attended took him aside and inquired whether he'd like to serve Allah in the most important way.

* * *

47

"You have been here many years, Mahmoud. You have done well, and it is time for you to serve our cause."

"What is it you wish me to do?"

"You will go on a very long journey." He looked into Mahmoud's eyes. "Perhaps not to come back. Are you ready for such a journey?"

Finally he had been called. Mahmoud nodded without a hint of hesitation.

"Pack your belongings, take them home to your family. Say good-bye and then come back to me. I will give you everything you need."

Mahmoud hurried to the small room he shared with his brother. He couldn't wait to tell Rashid, even though his heart suddenly felt heavy. What would his younger brother do without him?

Rashid was not in their room when he entered, and Mahmoud had never said good-bye.

⁕　　⁕　　⁕

MAHMOUD TOOK A PHOTO from a side pouch of the satchel. It showed him standing with his parents, sister, and brother in front of their shack. He wondered if Rashid missed him. The brothers had left home at ages 10 and nine, and in the past eight years, Mahmoud had often served as Rashid's parent.

Their father was a poor, illiterate goat herder far from a town with public schools. More than anything he had wanted his sons to be educated. While he had wished for an unrestricted education for them, a local madrassa had been the only choice. He had hugged each son tightly when he brought them to the school but had not said a word.

With the start of the Afghan jihad war with the Soviet Union, the madrassas in Pakistan had changed. Boosted by financial support from the Persian Gulf states, they became a recruiting ground for anti-Soviet mujahedin fighters.

Students learned basic math by counting hand grenades and dead Soviets.

After the fall of the Soviet Union, the focus of hatred in the madrassas shifted from that country to the West, and to the United States in particular. Patrons from the Gulf states advocated a strict form of Islam. They forbade the teaching of secular subjects, so Mahmoud and Rashid studied religious-based subjects centered on the Koran and other Islamic texts, as well as Arabic and some history. The brothers also had listened to motivational speeches that were filled with anti-materialistic, anti-Western, and anti-worldly sentiments. They spent their time between three meals and five prayer sessions a day sitting on thin carpets memorizing the Koran.

The "right" students, those who showed a willingness to embrace this extreme form of Islam, were selected to continue to a jihadist camp for further indoctrination and military training.

With its militant leanings, Mahmoud's madrassa became the perfect target for the Uktamiya, freedom fighters in Kyrgyzstan who had splintered from the Hizb ut-Tahrir, a radical Islamic movement in Uzbekistan. Funded by Afghan drug lords, the Uktamiya were intent on sending the United States a message—to stay out. The presence of a U.S. base in southern Kyrgyzstan and a planned anti-terrorist training camp had infuriated them. The radical group had infiltrated many madrassas to recruit help through their leaders who were paid handsomely to find willing jihadists.

Mahmoud's father had begged him not to go. He hadn't agreed with the direction the madrassa had taken and didn't trust the leaders. When Mahmoud said good-bye to his family, his father had grabbed him by the arms. Mahmoud had pushed him away. "I've been called upon," he'd said simply.

"No," his mother had cried. Mahmoud had ignored her.

But he took the photo his sister had pressed into his hands. He passed his fingers over the picture and replaced it in the satchel.

The donkey stumbled. "Stupid animal," the driver said, yanking on the reins.

Mahmoud felt sorry for the donkey. He felt sorry for his family, too. They had not understood. This was his chance to be part of an effort to return Islam to the world. He felt proud, believing he was depended upon by others to fulfill a mission and to achieve greatness. Perhaps in time, his family also would feel that way.

With a hand, Mahmoud shaded his face, the smooth skin barely scored by the start of a beard. He squinted at the dry rocky landscape and thought about the trip ahead. Later in the day, he'd arrive in Charsadda where he'd take a bus to Peshawar. There, he'd catch a train to Karachi where he'd be met and given further instructions.

He had never been to a place as large as Peshawar. He'd never been on a train. He had only heard about Karachi with its immorality and infidel influence. He didn't know what his future held. But he had no fear. Allah took all fear away. He squeezed the satchel that bulged with the Koran and with the rupees.

EIGHT

THE SIGN at the juncture of the side trail leading down to Echo Lake, just west of Lake Tahoe, couldn't have come soon enough. Sonora Pass, which Luke had been through several days ago, had signaled a change in the geology of the trail. The solid, durable granite of the High Sierras had given way to gentler volcanic mountains in the northern part of California, and the trail followed a route at a lower altitude, which meant fewer snowfields and creeks to cross. But 28-mile-days up and down gravelly volcanic ridges had tired him.

In the guidebook, he had read about Papa Quail, a trail angel near Echo Lake. On the PCT, trail angels, who also sported trail names, were often the life blood for thru-hikers. Some drove hours over rough roads to leave jugs of water at particularly dry sections. Others set up barbecues out of their cars at a cold mountain pass. Still others, like Papa Quail, invited hikers into their homes, offering showers, dinner, and a good night's rest. A place to recoup from injuries, too. At this point on the trail, hikers pressed themselves to do 30-mile-days to stick to their schedules, a pace that often brought on stress fractures and back injuries. Hikers could be laid up at a trail angel's place for days.

Papa Quail was renowned up and down the trail for his hospitality. Twice a day, every day during the hiking season, he waited at the parking lot near the Echo Lake Resort Post Office to pick up hikers and take them to his home near the lake. He'd also drive them to South Lake Tahoe where they could enjoy the endless buffets at the gambling casinos across the Nevada border. Luke had heard how dangerous the buffets could be. Eating even a little of the rich food after living on hiker fare forced many would-be feasters outside to vomit in the trash dumpsters. He planned to avoid that fate.

Luke turned the corner into the parking lot. It was nearly 4:30, and he was late for the pickup, which the guidebook said occurred around 4 P.M. He didn't want to camp for the night and considered calling Papa Quail. To his relief, a truck with a California quail painted on the door was still there. No other hikers were around. The truck door opened and a large, square man wearing a cowboy hat got out. "I'm Papa Quail," he said, extending his hand.

Luke took Papa Quail's hand and felt the strong grip of a confident man.

"Thanks for waiting," said Luke. He dumped his pack in the back of the truck and climbed into the cab. "Is the post office still open? I should have a box there."

"Sure," replied Papa Quail. "It's just down the road."

"Where's everyone else?" asked Luke.

"They're back at the house," replied Papa Quail. "I got dinner ready early, so thought I'd check the parking lot one last time."

Luke discerned a slight Slavic accent. Eastern European, he thought. He looked at Papa Quail again and found the trail angel returning his gaze. There was no mistaking a feeling of connection. Had he been waiting for Luke? But for what?

Luke settled back into the seat. *You're out of the Bureau. Don't be paranoid.*

"There aren't many hikers there just now," Papa Quail continued, "plenty of room in the trailer."

"That'll be a nice change from a tent."

They drove down a dirt road to the post office where a resupply box from Marina waited for him. Then they headed toward the lake.

Papa Quail glanced at Luke, then back at the road. "You doing the whole trail?" he asked.

"Trying to," said Luke. He got the feeling the trail angel was inspecting him.

"Not too many go it alone," said Papa Quail. "You don't mind?"

"No," replied Luke, "When I was a kid, I used to spend a lot of time alone in the north woods of Wisconsin. My granddad and I would fish and camp for a few days, and then he'd leave. I had to find my way home. These days some people might call that abusive, but I thought it was fun."

"You're not from this country?" It was Luke's turn to ask a question.

"Poland originally," replied Papa Quail. "I hiked always in the Tatra Mountains. I immigrated here in the 60s, cooked in a Chicago restaurant for a while, and met my wife there. But I missed the mountains and got into software programming in Silicon Valley just at the right time. And so here we are."

He patted his girth. "As you can see, I don't do much hiking now. But I like to help. I like to be a part of such a walk."

"I don't know what we'd do without you guys."

"My wife isn't so happy with the house full of scruffy hikers, so she spends a couple of months in the summer with her sister in San Francisco."

"Tonight it's ribs," he continued. "I assume you're hungry?"

"Famished," replied Luke.

Papa Quail's place was nestled among tall pines near Echo Lake. It was a plain, two-story clapboard house but with a large deck overlooking the lake. Papa Quail showed Luke to his bunk in a trailer just outside the house and pointed the way to the towels and shower. "Don't forget the message board next to the shower."

Then he turned to the half dozen men and women swimming in front of the house.

"Dinner in an hour," he called, and left Luke to wash up.

Luke gathered his dirty laundry and a change of clothes and headed for the shower. He stopped at the board covered with notes and was pleased to find one posted to him from Sea Dog. He had already passed through Lake Tahoe, the note said, eaten too much at a casino buffet and visited the dumpster out back—but not before recouping the money he'd spent at the buffet at the $5 slots—and was planning to get off the trail again at Belden. "Catch up, Camper," the note had ended. Luke smiled, remembering the SEAL's pace. *Yeah, right.* He started a laundry and headed into the shower.

Dinner was served at the picnic table outside the house. Luke chewed on messy ribs, buttery corn on the cob, salad, and the softest rolls he'd ever bit into. He didn't think he'd ever tasted anything so good. While he ate, he listened to the other hikers recount their latest trail adventures. One had gotten a ride into a town from a hermit who hadn't left the mountains for a couple of years. Another had nearly sat on a rattlesnake.

After they washed up, they gathered in Papa Quail's living room for more stories. Papa Quail laughed at every other sentence, clearly enjoying the company.

Slouched against the wall, a bearded hiker stared silently at the chattering group. Despite a week of sunny days, his cheeks were sunken, his skin sallow. He had already downed a couple of beers and was on his third. Luke guessed he was on the trail to unload some demons, like many hikers—maybe like himself. But this fellow didn't appear to be doing such a great job. *He looks like shit.* Despite a loss of 30 pounds, Luke hoped he didn't look as bad.

Luke turned to him. "Where you from?"

"Georgia," came the reply and nothing else.

Luke quit the conversation.

He grabbed a beer and sat next to a couple of girls so tattooed not much skin showed. He chanced conversation again.

"You girls doing the whole trail?"

"No, just California this year," one replied.

"Nice," Luke found himself stumbling with words, but continued. "Where are you from?"

"We work in human resources for a company in Ashland. Had enough of it for a while. Wanted to do something different. How about you?"

"I just retired and thought I'd do the trail."

The girls nodded. "Way to go. Good for you."

Their reply somehow made Luke feel old.

"Where do you live?" the one with the lip ring asked.

"Southern California, about an hour north of L.A."

"We love the weather down there—compared to Ashland, it's heaven. But the snakes. Tina got a picture of one sleeping right in the middle of the trail!"

"Yeah, they're hard to see," said Luke.

They talked a while longer about animals, the weather, and the culture of Southern California, but instead of focusing on the conversation, Luke found himself worrying about his own daughters' potential penchant for body art.

A loud wheezing noise turned their attention to Papa Quail, who had pulled out an accordion. Even though the group didn't know Polish, they sang along anyway as Papa Quail serenaded them with Polish folk songs.

Luke listened, drinking his beer. He felt stupid thinking that this jolly, loud singer had been waiting for him at the trail head.

His enjoyment of the entertainment was short-lived as exhaustion set in. He raised his beer to Papa Quail and left for the trailer. He found he had a decent cell phone signal and called Marina.

"Hey, Mari, I'm at Lake Tahoe at a trail angel's," he said when she picked up.

"Oh, hi, Luke," came the reply. "I'm just on my way out the door to get the girls. They're over at the Franklins. Did you get the re-supply box?"

Luke heard the curt tone—again. No asking how he was. How the hike was going.

"Yes, it's here. Thanks. You okay?" he added. "You sound in a hurry."

He heard her take a deep breath, like she was trying to control herself.

"I'm fine, Luke, it's just that the girls are waiting for me. Oh, you'll never guess who called. Gennady Zukov. It's been ages since we've heard from them. They're all well, Sasha is still playing tennis."

"He said to say hello to you," she added. "He sounded glad you were on the trail."

"Thanks, Mari," said Luke. "Say hi to the girls. I miss you all."

"We miss you, too." Marina hung up.

Luke lay on the bed. It'd been a long time since they had heard from the Zukovs. His old adversary had loved the mountains. He'd have to make sure he sent a postcard when he came to the next town. A funny, nagging feeling crept into his chest. *Jesus, you are getting paranoid.* He turned on his side and in a moment, he was asleep.

The next morning, Luke re-packed his backpack with clean clothes and the new supplies. Then he stripped the bed and followed the smell of bacon to the kitchen.

After a breakfast of pancakes, bacon, and eggs, Papa Quail drove the hikers back to the parking lot. The beer-drinker wasn't among them. *Looks like he's planning to treat Papa Quail with his smile for another few days,* thought Luke. *These trail angels are saints.* Luke tucked a $20 bill under Papa Quail's gloves in the front seat of the truck before they piled in—a small payment for all he did.

At the parking lot, the hikers slung on their packs and shook hands with the trail angel.

"Hey, Camper," Papa Quail called as they headed toward the trail, "I almost forgot. I've got something for you."

Luke turned back to the truck, thinking the money had been found and not wanted. Papa Quail's demeanor had completely changed. The smile was gone. He leaned out of the cab's window. "I have a message for you," he said quietly.

Luke's heart skipped a beat.

"When you reach Aloha Lake, look for a man fishing. He needs to talk to you."

Before Luke could respond, Papa Quail shifted into first gear and drove away.

Luke watched the truck roll out of the parking lot. He felt his gut twist.

NINE

A FEW HOURS out of Echo Lake, Luke entered Desolation Wilderness. Glaciers had dug out hundreds of lakes, but left behind rocky soil in which few trees were able to take hold and grow. The lakes still overflowed from snowmelt and flooded the trail. Luke worked his way on and off the trail, which ran close to the water, disappeared, then reappeared several yards later. Mosquitoes, not a problem until now, attacked even the smallest patch of exposed skin not smeared in DEET. Their insistent buzzing infringed on the eerie stillness.

As Luke walked past the glassy pools, the pieces of information he'd gotten at Echo Lake spun in his head. He tried to dismiss them as coincidence, but they didn't add up. First, there was the call from Gennady, then that cryptic remark from Papa Quail to look for a fisherman at Aloha Lake. Could Gennady have something to do with that? Twenty years as an investigator had bent his brain so that very little turned out to be coincidental. Something was up, and the last thing he wanted—or needed—was to be involved in the business again.

59

Luke stopped at one of the pools and studied his reflection in it. Though slightly thinner, a calm face looked back at him, one with the same dark, intense eyes that bespoke a career driven by an exceptional single-mindedness. It hadn't been all bad, he knew that. In fact, he'd had many fulfilling and interesting cases. There was the reactive work that had started his career in Baltimore where he and his wild partner, Jake, went after bank robbers. Luke chuckled at the memory. Jake, a Vietnam War veteran, had already shot two people by the time Luke arrived. One more and he'd have gone to the applicant squad where he wouldn't pull a pistol from his holster again. Luke had served as point man on arrests, always going first through a door or into a building, while Jake stayed at the back. He also was the designated driver, ensuring that his heavy-drinking partner reached home without incident after the squad's Wednesday happy hour.

After Baltimore, the work turned out to be unexpectedly challenging and fortuitous. In the 80s, there was the Zukov spy case in New York that garnered some pretty nice kudos. At the Newark office, he ran a counterterrorism squad when CT wasn't sexy and became the lead investigator for the 1993 bombing of the World Trade Centers. At L.A., he was promoted to Assistant Special Agent in Charge of the counterterrorism and counterintelligence programs. With large populations of Chinese, Iranian, Afghan, and Korean residents in the L.A. area, there was plenty of work assessing threats and helping the CIA identify sources of information. In L.A., he'd gotten in on the ground floor of an upcoming focus of the FBI—weapons of mass destruction. Every other week, he attended a possible WMD crime scene with the FBI's Hazmat and WMD squads. He'd been busy.

Luke picked up a flat stone and skimmed it across the water. Looking back, he knew he'd done the country some good.

But the Bureau's tendency for blaming the wrong people and sacrificing substance had stolen his pride and left him with a sense of failure instead of satisfaction. The Trina Kim case had affected him, but many other instances had taken down a lot of good agents. Like Scotty Dunn, who'd been forced to testify at a congressional hearing because his supervisors didn't care to face difficult questions. Scotty had taken the brunt of questions that should have been lobbed at higher level people. He'd never gotten over it and left the Bureau. What had happened to the Bureau's core values of fairness, integrity, accountability, and leadership? He'd seen little of it, especially during the last years of his career. The great FBI, the organization he'd admired as a child on the news, on TV, and in movies, was, to him now, a fraud. Its director nothing more than a bureaucrat who spent his time flying around in the FBI's private jet, like some sort of CEO, leaving his deputy to appoint worthless cronies to key positions throughout the organization.

Luke picked up another stone, this time throwing it as hard as he could. He followed its arc through the air ar heard it split the water open. He watched ripples carry water, and his thoughts, outward. He continued alon trail and followed it to the southern tip of Aloha Lake just as Papa Quail had described—a fisherman ov old worn gear with a cap drawn low over his bro' ing near the shore. He glanced at Luke, then gaze to the lake, swatting at mosquitoes. Lu' was tall and middle-aged under the shabby

Luke looked around. They were alone. back, the same feeling he'd had just befo' Was this some sort of set-up by Luke'? loyalty check? Had they intercepte' rina? He felt for his tomahawk a'

Though he had often taken down rabbits for dinner as a teen, he'd never thrown his tomahawk at a human being. He wondered if he could.

Luke walked cautiously toward the man. "How's the fishing?"

"Not so good," replied the fisherman, surveying Luke. He took in every detail of Luke, as Luke had done him. He began winding in his line. "You look much thinner than Gennady described."

Luke discerned the same Slavic accent and soft voice of Papa Quail's. He didn't reply. He kept his hand on the tomahawk.

The fisherman put one hand up, reassuring Luke. With the other, he reached into his pocket and slowly withdrew a key ring. On the end was a round metal charm. Luke immediately recognized it as the charm he'd found when searching Gennady's apartment in the Bronx after his arrest. He had returned it to Gennady before his departure from the country. Ironically, the charm was a crudely stamped FBI medallion, the sort of thing commonly sold to tourists on the streets of New York City.

This guy knew who Luke was.

"I've got a message from Gennady. Trusted sources have told him a network of terrorist cells is transporting pieces of a dirty bomb out of Russia. They don't know where, but obviously the United States is a likely target."

Luke stared at the fisherman. "What are you talking about? Who are you?"

The fisherman began packing up his gear. "He says you'll ow what to do. He says to remember Veronika's face."

Wait." Luke grabbed his shoulder. But the man shoved 's hand away. "That's all I have to tell you." He held up nd to stop any further conversation and hurried down away from the lake.

Luke knew better than to try to stop him. Or follow. He took off his pack and sat on a log near the shore. He had to get himself together. His first reaction was to dismiss Gennady's message as imaginative foolery. Too many hours in Moscow State's dull Engineering Building. He must still miss the hunt.

But then there was Veronika. Veronika's face. The mention of Gennady's dead daughter brought gravity to the message. When Gennady lived in New York, Luke had closely followed the Zukovs in an unmarked government car all over the boroughs as they did their errands. Bumper-lock surveillance provided a way to tell a target that U.S. intelligence was on to them. It also let the target know the identity of a counterintelligence officer, in the event he might want to "talk" about anything. As Luke drove behind, Veronika would look out the back window of their car, scrunch up her face and stick out her tongue. It had been tough not to smile back. Luke remembered visiting Veronika at the Cancer Center. As weak as she was, she stuck out her tongue at him.

There was no question in Luke's mind that Gennady's message was real. He thought back to his conversation with Marina. When had Gennady called her—maybe a week ago? He must have acted fast. Found a network of spies still in place, and in just two weeks managed to get a message out. There must still be a web of Russian spies in the U.S. At least retired ones who owed Gennady something. Why would Gennady get involved in this? He wouldn't, unless it threatened his beloved Russia.

Luke put on his pack and slowly walked along Aloha Lake. What could he do even if the intelligence was good? He was in the middle of nowhere for Christ's sake. Let someone else investigate—for a change. Maybe that was what Gennady intended. Maybe he just wanted Luke to alert the right people. Trouble was, there were no longer many right people in the

Bureau. Nor would anyone listen to him after his abrupt and less-than-friendly departure. If anyone did have a conversation with Luke, they'd be in danger of having their career derailed.

A dog's bark brought Luke out of his thoughts. Ahead he found a young, wiry, pony-tailed hiker resting with his dog. "Hey," said the hiker, looking up at Luke.

"Hey," returned Luke. "Nice dog."

Luke liked dogs but hadn't wanted one while he and his family lived in small houses with yards the size of a couple of cars. Leashes and poop-scoopers weren't his idea of living with a dog. It had been an issue with the twins who, for years, had begged for a puppy. Instead, they'd had the usual assortment of hamsters and a couple of cats, which had placated Carrie and Grace, but not succeeded as a substitute for a dog.

"Thanks. I'm Aimless. This is Mutt."

Mutt, a medium-sized, mixed breed, wagged his tail. Luke scratched his head.

"I'm Camper." He pointed to his large pack, which he began to take off.

Aimless raised his eyebrows at the sight of the pack being unloaded from Luke's back.

Luke noticed the slight build of Aimless—another ultralight hiker. He pulled out lunch, knowing the answer to what he was about to ask. "Want some? I've got plenty."

"Sure," said Aimless and helped himself to sandwiches Luke had made before leaving Echo Lake.

"Where you from?" asked Luke, happy to be distracted.

"Here and there," replied Aimless. He swallowed huge pieces of a bologna sandwich and washed it down with water. "Mutt and I are heading up to Canada, then turning back down the trail to Oregon. My grandmother lives there."

He tossed scraps of bread to Mutt. "That's as far as I've gotten in my plans."

"You got a real name?"

"No," answered Aimless. "I've got no identity."

"What do you mean?"

Aimless grinned at Luke's puzzled expression. "Nothing. No passport. No driver's license, no credit cards. My parents even burned my birth certificate. They didn't want their privacy invaded by technology. Luddites to the extreme, you might say. So I'm just aimless. Never been to school, never been fingerprinted, or photographed. I don't have a social security number. I don't exist. And I like it that way."

Luke just nodded. By now, he was accustomed to meeting unusual people on the trail. Supergirl was a personal trainer from Alabama. She claimed she should have been born a man. Yo-Yo was going up the trail and back down in one year. And this was his third year doing so. Nowhere Man had said God sent him to walk the trail. Now Aimless.

"What about you?" asked Aimless, "What do you do?"

"I'm retired," answered Luke.

"You look kind of young to be retired," said Aimless.

"I got out of the rat race early."

"Feels good, doesn't it," said Aimless.

Luke thought about the wisdom of those words. "Yeah, it does."

After he and Aimless finished Luke's lunch, they looked at the next section in the guide and discussed what lay ahead—namely, the halfway mark.

"We're nearly there." Aimless shouldered his small pack. "Thanks for the food."

He whistled for Mutt. "See you up the trail."

Then he turned back to Luke with a sympathetic smile. "Man, you've got to do something about that big pack you carry."

Luke watched Aimless and Mutt disappear around a bend. He leaned against a massive lodge pole pine. He closed his eyes and soaked up the smell of the pine needles. But like earwigs, Gennady's message dug into the silence. *You'll know what to do.*

TEN

MAHMOUD STARTED awake to the noise of people talking and rummaging for their luggage. Across from him, the girl who had spoken to him earlier held her mother's hand and waved good-bye.

The journey from Peshawar had taken 12 hours. In the cushioned seats even economy class afforded, he had slept most of the way, interrupted only by a family of three who had boarded shortly after Peshawar and settled in seats next to him. Mahmoud had opened his eyes and nodded. The couple's young girl had smiled at Mahmoud and offered him a biscuit. "Have one," she said. Though Mahmoud was wary, her shy smile and innocent eyes had reminded him of his sister and he had accepted. The biscuit tasted foreign, but delicious.

Mahmoud waved back, motioning slightly with his fingers. He found his satchel and followed the other passengers from the train. When he stepped into glaring sunlight at the Karachi station, he was assaulted by the polluted air. He coughed and rubbed his eyes and could only squint at the swarm of people covering the train platform.

He had been told to walk to the station where he'd be met by someone trustworthy. Still coughing, Mahmoud followed the mass of people flowing toward the main station. He was unprepared for what engulfed him. Besides Urdu, his language, people were calling to each other in Sinahi, Punjabi, Pashto, and Balochi. He was bumped and jostled by men and women hurrying by—dark- and light-skinned people in traditional Pakistani clothing but also in blue jeans and T-shirts, skirts, and dresses. He'd never been confronted by such a mélange of faces and clothing. Nor had he heard such a jumble of languages. He held his satchel closely.

At the station door, someone grabbed his arm. Mahmoud jerked it away, losing his balance. He fell into a traveler who shoved him aside. He stumbled and nearly dropped the satchel.

"Mahmoud, Mahmoud," a quiet voice said.

Mahmoud spun around.

"It's alright." The man touched only his shoulder this time. "Come with me."

He guided Mahmoud through the sea of people to the back of the station where a car waited. He opened the back door, and they got inside.

Mahmoud looked at the small man, dressed in a salwar kameez. He had a moustache, but not a beard. His eyes were friendly, his smile quick.

"How did you know it was me?" he asked.

"Easy," replied the man, laughing. "You were coughing from the air pollution. Only people from the country do that." He winked. "I am Jafar. That is Nadir." He pointed to the driver, who did not respond. Instead, the heavy-set man looked in the rear-view mirror.

"We are glad to see you. We have been waiting. How was your journey?"

"It was fine. Where are we going?"

"To a safe place," replied Jafar. "Do not worry. This is an overwhelming city for a newcomer. We will take care of you."

As the car pulled away from the station, Jafar settled into the back seat and motioned for Mahmoud to do the same.

Mahmoud shivered. "It's cold."

"Air conditioning," explained his companion.

Nadir again checked the rear- and side-view mirrors and then pulled out into the street.

"Look, Mahmoud," said Jafar, "look out the window. We will take you the long way so you can see our city of lights."

The car wove slowly through Karachi. The city was hectic and noisy, the streets full of buses, cars, motorcycles, and carts. A cosmopolitan mix of people from all over Pakistan, and from neighboring countries, jammed the sidewalks. Mahmoud couldn't take his eyes off them.

He stared wide-eyed at the startling mixture of old and new juxtaposed close to one another—ancient mosques and asphalt bypasses, Gothic churches and tall skyscrapers, Italian Renaissance and modern Islamic buildings. Though he tried not to show it, Mahmoud was spellbound.

He noticed that the car passed the same building several times and that Nadir glanced often in the car's mirrors. "Why do we go around the same streets?" he asked.

"People watch us," replied Jafar. "We want to be sure they don't follow."

Before Mahmoud could ask why, Nadir slowed the car and spoke for the first time since they'd left the train station.

"That is the mausoleum of Quaid e Azam," he said.

Mahmoud looked intently at the mausoleum of Pakistan's revered founder and its first governor general. The white marble building shone in the sun. The gardens surrounding the site were calm and tranquil, dotted with palm trees, fountains, and flowering shrubs. Dogs roamed the area, and they looked well fed. He felt a stab of homesickness. As a boy, he'd had a dog, Mothi. On many days, while tending goats far in the hills behind his home, Mothi had been his only companion. The loyal dog had walked the perimeter of the herd by his side, had found strays, and rescued babies who'd gotten stuck among rocks. He had laid his head on Mahmoud's lap when there was only resting to do. Mothi had been a good friend.

"Who owns those dogs?" he asked.

"Ah, they are all strays," replied Jafar. "People leave food for them. The mayor's wife has decreed that they cannot be killed." He shrugged his shoulders.

At the famous Empress Market, they stopped for something to eat. The town markets where Mahmoud and his father sold goat milk were pitiful in comparison. Over 200 shops and stalls filled the old market building. Mahmoud had never seen nor smelled so many different kinds of food. Whole sides of meat hung row after row, fish of all shapes and sizes layered tables, vegetables and fruits whose names he did not know rose in pyramids, colorful bags of grains crowded the floors. But it was the Peshawari Ice Cream Parlour that most astounded him. The soft, sweet, cold substance filled his mouth and in an instant, was gone. Jafar laughed at the look of surprise and delight on his face as he spooned it in again and again. It was a bowl of ice cream that he brought back to the car.

Mahmoud was scraping the bowl with his spoon when the car lurched. His head banged against the back of the front seat. Nadir careened around a corner. Mahmoud gripped the edge of his seat.

He looked at Jafar. "What are you doing?"

Jafar didn't answer. He glanced out the back window. All traces of good humor had left his face. "Get rid of them," he ordered Nadir.

Nadir wrenched the steering wheel to the left and they careened down a narrow side street. Mahmoud clung to whatever he could as the car rocked to one side of the street, then the other. Pedestrians hurried to step out of the way. After several more heart-stopping turns, Nadir steadied the car.

Jafar turned to Mahmoud. "Police Special Branches," he said. "They try to follow us, but they don't know the streets as well."

"Why do they follow you?" asked Mahmoud when his heart had slowed.

"They look for those of us who want to save them. They want to break apart our network. They don't understand." answered Jafar.

"We help our brothers who fight the jihad elsewhere," he continued. "They come here to rest and find medical treatment for their wounds. We give them money and arms. The Police Special Branches try to find them. They send drones to kill them. But we hide them well."

"Drones?" asked Mahmoud.

"Yes, drones. Small, clever planes that fly with no pilot." He spoke patiently, as if Mahmoud were a small child. "They are built in the United States and see from far up in the sky where we cannot reach them. They shoot missiles through windows into homes. The CIA and our own government kill many of our women and children this way."

Mahmoud fell silent. He had never heard of such technology. Machines that killed so accurately and quickly. He had not heard of many things, he realized as they left the distinctive buildings of Karachi behind and headed south toward the port.

"Your tour is over," Jafar said. "Time for business. We are going to Manora now, Mahmoud. It will be safe there, and you will get new directions."

Mahmoud nodded and watched the scenery change from busy streets to dilapidated and poor settlements. They turned onto a road that led to Karachi's waterfront. As they passed the harbor, he could see beyond the ships and fishing boats to a wide stretch of water.

"You've never seen the ocean." It was a statement, not a question.

"No," replied Mahmoud, shaking his head. "No."

"Some people like it," said Jafar. "Some people don't. You will see. You are going to learn all about fishing."

This was the first hint as to where Mahmoud was going next. Out to sea. He saw that Jafar watched him closely for his reaction. He did not want to show any hesitation, any fear, and kept his features still.

They crossed a narrow causeway that led onto an island. Soon they passed a tall lighthouse. "It lights the way for ships coming into the harbor," explained Jafar.

Nadir stopped the car just past the lighthouse.

"See that plaque?" said Jafar. "It says 'Warning: from May to August, the sea swallows every living being.'"

Mahmoud could not help himself. His eyes widened. Jafar and Nadir laughed.

"On this island used to be the main base of the Pakistan Navy," explained Jafar. "But the ships have moved to another location. Manora is mostly fishing villages and beaches now. A company from Dubai has bought much of the land here, to build hotels, condos, restaurants, and clubs. It is not right that this should happen." He rolled down the window and spat.

It was nearly evening when they reached a small village at the end of the island. They stopped along a stretch of beach and motioned for Mahmoud to get out. He took his sandals off and walked through the sand. It stuck between his toes, gritty and soft at the same time. Above him, seagulls squawked. He waded into the salty water, and cupped some in his hands. He sipped it, then coughed.

He gazed at the Arabian Sea. The flatness and openness to the horizon filled him with deep emotion. Was it awe? Fear? Or was it the realization that he was a small part of something so enormous?

He prayed silently.

"Come, Mahmoud," shouted Jafar. "Our leader is anxious to meet you."

Mahmoud turned from the sea. On an impulse, he ran through the sand all the way back to the car.

ELEVEN

MARINA HESITATED before opening the gate to Charlie and Peg Logan's back yard. It was nearly 90 degrees, and the space was already packed with people, some gathered around the pool, others relaxing in lounge chairs under umbrellas. Palm, lemon, and orange trees edged the yard. In between the trees grew succulents and bird-of-paradise flowers. With bougainvillea tumbling over the wall behind the pool, the area gave off a lively, tropical feeling. She inhaled the heavenly perfume of the blossoms framing the gate.

Marina spotted the usual suspects, mostly members of the L.A. Joint Terrorism Task Force, the JTTF, which Luke had overseen, and which Charlie now headed. Facing them brought back feelings of anger and disappointment at how Luke had been treated at the end of his career, and what it was doing to her marriage—his stand against taking a good security job, his let's-return-to-the-woods attitude.

Also present were people from Alcohol, Tobacco and Firearms; Immigration and Customs Enforcement; and supervisors from the FBI's counterterrorism squads; as well as the L.A.

75

sheriff and LAPD detectives. A real who's who of law enforcement. And there was Ken Savage, an Inspector General for the U.S. Justice Department whom Luke had admired and worked with. *Well, Charlie is a trusted, likable guy. He knows how to get everybody together.*

Next to a table set up as a bar, Dirk Barnstable, L.A.'s counterterrorism supervisor, was downing beers with one of the bomb techs. Marina didn't recognize his latest conquest. From the looks of her defined arms and flat midriff, she likely worked out at the same gym he frequented. Absent from the group was Jen Johnson, the special agent in charge of the L.A. division. It's early yet, Marina knew. Jen would stop by to show her support, then make an excuse about having to get ready for an important trip.

Marina relaxed a little when she saw a few non-law enforcement guests talking together. Someone to sit next to, since no one from the Bureau would make an effort to talk to her. When Luke had retired under less-than-pleasant circumstances, she also was ostracized. Agents' wives who'd once been friends no longer were. Invitations to Bureau parties were nonexistent. Thank God for Charlie and Peg. Despite Luke's situation, they had remained good friends.

Even with Charlie and Peg's loyalty, she hadn't wanted to come to the barbecue, but her daughters, Carrie and Grace, had insisted. Get out of the house for a while, they'd said. She had capitulated but wasn't so sure she should have.

Marina pushed open the gate. Carrie and Grace crowded by. "Look at their pool!" said Carrie. Matt, Charlie and Peg's son, waved to them from a crowd of teens splashing and throwing balls.

"We're hitting the water," said Grace. She and her sister sauntered, hips swinging, toward the Logan's pool at one end of the yard.

"Hey, my mermaid." Marina felt a huge pair of arms wrap around her from behind and lift her off the ground. It was Leon Malone. She knew from the size of the arms even before she heard his deep voice. She squirmed around to face him. "Leon!" she exclaimed. "I'm so glad to see you, but I thought you'd be on some deep-sea fishing adventure. Luke said that's about all you do since you retired."

Leon released Marina and grinned. "He's right about that, but now and then I have to come back to shore. To fuel up, at least. My boat is my new lady friend. You'll have to meet her—she's not like the others." He laughed heartily.

Marina saw that Leon hadn't changed a bit since he retired from the JTTF a couple of years ago. The same crew cut, narrow blue eyes, and wizened skin of someone who spent time in the sun. Still a bear of a man with the strength and voice to match. He'd been with the L.A. Police Department assigned to the JTTF, a man Luke had trusted, she knew. He couldn't wait to retire, buy a boat, and fish. And he did. He looked happy.

He reached for an appetizer from a plate Marina held. "I'm getting a beer to go with these. Catch you later. I want to hear all about Luke's hike."

"Okay, Leon," said Marina. She watched him head for the bar.

Marina waved to Charlie, who was grilling a mountain of burgers and dogs. He smiled and waved a mitted hand back. *They are such a great couple*, Marina thought. Charlie—short, with twinkling eyes and a loud laugh. Peg—taller than her husband, slender with blond cropped hair. She wore classic, sporty clothing and looked like she stepped out of a Talbot's catalogue. They went together like pieces of a jigsaw puzzle.

Marina adjusted her sunglasses and smoothed her hair, then made her way to a table where Peg was arranging food. She was a professional decorator and it showed. The tablecloth spoke country French, bright yellow with swirls of red and green twisting in it. Green paper napkins and cups, and flatware with green plastic handles accented the colors. *Martha Stewart has nothing on Peg,* Marina mused.

"Hi, Peg," she said giving the hostess a hug. "Everything looks so nice. What a beautiful tablecloth."

"Hi, Marina. You know me, I can't resist linens." Peg put a hand on Marina's shoulder. "I'm glad you decided to come this year."

"Oh, I didn't want to miss Charlie's famous burgers," said Marina. "And the girls love your new pool. I'm tempted to try out that rock slide myself."

"We'll definitely do a ladies-only party before the summer ends."

Marina handed her hostess a plate. "My usual—curry cheese crackers. You know I bring them everywhere."

"I'm glad you did. Everybody loves those. Thanks, Marina."

Peg poured them each a glass of prosecco. "You like this, don't you?"

"I sure do," replied Marina, clinking Peg's glass. "I remember you introduced us to it when you returned from your Italy trip."

Marina looked toward the pool. "Matt's having fun with the girls."

"Yes, but he probably wishes he were a bit older. He's always liked your daughters."

"They're good kids. We're lucky."

Peg looked directly at Marina. "How's it going without Luke?" Peg asked. "I'm sorry I haven't been around to do more things with you. This decorating job in Santa •Barbara was more than I bargained for."

"Oh, I'm doing alright, Peg. The girls have part-time jobs at the movie theater, and between that and tennis lessons, I'm pretty busy driving them around. I'm glad to have the summer off though. It was hectic for a while when school was still going. I've got some time to get out more with the run club in Camarillo."

"What do you hear from Luke?"

"He's nearly at the halfway mark, Peg. I never doubted his success, really, barring a fall or bout of giardia."

"Wow! Halfway. Good for him."

"Yes, good for him, but the sooner he gets back to reality, the better. He's got to settle down. I'm looking forward to our future, but he seems to want to go backwards, back to the woods of Wisconsin." Marina twisted the stem of her glass. "I won't live in a cabin, Peg."

Peg put an arm around Marina's shoulder. "Luke will realize he needs to get a job, Marina. He knows the sacrifices you've made over the past 20 years. Let him go through this de-stressing time. It'll be a good way for him to let go of those last few years in the Bureau. Then he'll be more open to your plans."

"My plans?"

"You know, to train as an OR nurse. Doesn't he support that?"

"Yes, I think so." Marina stared at the bubbles breaking the surface of her wine.

"I'm really not sure he even remembers my plans, Peg. These past few years have all but consumed him. He's made it to most of the girls' tennis matches, but that's about all."

She looked up at her friend. "He certainly doesn't support my desire to stay in this area. I don't want to be in the country. I don't want that kind of life. I want to work at a busy hospital where I can get lots of experience every day. I want to be near friends. And, at the risk of sounding shallow, I want this...a nice house and a pool. Is that asking too much?"

"No, it's not," replied Peg.

Peg glanced at Charlie. "Look at him. He loves to grill." She wrinkled her nose. "But he burns the burgers every time."

Marina smiled. She noticed a young Asian woman walk toward Charlie. "Who's that?"

"Oh, that's Terri Densmore. She's a new analyst. Real sharp. I guess you haven't met her, though she worked a little with Luke. I'll be sure to introduce you later. She's a birdwatcher, like you."

Charlie and Terri engaged closely in conversation. Terri's head was bent, as if she couldn't hear what Charlie was saying to her. She looked very serious.

"She seems a little tense, for a party," said Marina.

"She does," Peg agreed, "but you know how Charlie loves to talk shop, and he thinks Terri is a great addition to the office."

Charlie signaled Peg with his spatula.

"Looks like the meeting is over. Time to eat," said Peg. "Why don't you gather up the kids, and I'll call the rest."

TWELVE

A T THE JUNCTION of the Mt. Jordan loop trail near the Donner Pass, Luke stopped and took his guide and map from his pack. For the time being, he'd pushed the fisherman's message from Gennady about dirty bombs out of his head. He wanted to enjoy the area. He consulted the map and considered whether or not to go the extra 1½ miles out of his way to catch the view of Donner Lake. On such a warm day, Luke found it hard to imagine that the peaceful, scenic area around this gentle mountain saddle was the site of one of the most famous disasters in American history.

Luke read in the guide that a popular memorial to the ill-fated Donner Party had opened just a few miles down Old Highway 40. Maybe he'd skip the loop and hitch a ride to the memorial instead.

Another 50 yards up the trail offered a good place to stop and eat, but when Luke reached the flat, shaded area, it was filled with horseback riders. Horses were common on the PCT, and while hikers complained about picking their way through dung-covered trails, they also realized the horseback riders and pack train operators did a lot of trail maintenance, including bridge building and boulder removal. No one complained too much.

Luke found a spot out of the group's way and took off his pack. Lunch was the usual jerky, trail mix, and a Snickers bar. He nodded hello to the riders.

An older, slender woman smiled in return. "You look like you're doing the whole trail."

Luke wondered how she came to that conclusion. His pack size? Scruffy look? Did he smell?

Luke studied her own elegant outfit—a split riding skirt, Spanish riding hat, expensive leather boots, a cream silk shirt, and leather gloves. She reminded him of Barbara Stanwyck's Victoria Barkley on the 60s TV show "The Big Valley."

Luke also noticed a young girl slumped on a nearby log. Her purple-tinged hair and black-colored lips contrasted sharply with "Barbara Stanwyck."

"Trying," he replied. "Some days I wouldn't mind having one of those horses."

"They're handy when it comes to carrying gear, that's true," replied the woman.

Luke took out his map. "I was thinking of hitching to the Pioneer Memorial near the lake."

"It's definitely worth it, if you've got the time," replied the woman. "The museum has exhibits on Native Americans and the transcontinental railroad, as well as the Donner Party." Her voice took on a somber tone. "I've just spent a few days showing my granddaughter, Vanessa, the area. We've ridden and camped all through the state park. What's left of one of the Donner Party's settlements is just behind the museum. "

She looked at her granddaughter. "I wanted Vanessa to see for herself."

One of the woman's other companions, a burly bodyguard type, explained. "This woman is Marion Reed, a descendent of one of the families who started with the Donners, but stayed east of the Sierras until spring."

Marion nodded. "My great-great-grandfather was in one of the relief parties that rescued them," she said. "He didn't want to let them down and went in on snowshoes as soon as he could."

"So he found them, didn't he?" asked Luke.

"Yes," said Marion. She stood as the group began to pack up the horses. "But by then only a few were alive. And some of those didn't make it to Sacramento."

"That's quite a legacy to carry," said Luke.

"I try to keep it going," replied Marion. "I was able to start up The Reed Rescue Force, a mountain rescue team that helps stranded hikers, or anyone who's lost."

"I've read about them," said Luke. "They'll go anywhere in any type of weather. They're extraordinary."

"Yes, they are just that. Real heroes." Marion swung onto her horse. She waved and turned up the trail.

Luke sat a few minutes longer pondering the Donner Party and Marion's words. Resentment rose to his throat. The mysterious fisherman's words stuck there: *He says you'll know what to do.* The words of Marion Reed's great-great-grandfather stuck there too: *He couldn't let them down.*

Can't let who down? Just as he was regaining his soul, he was being asked to risk it. And for what? What? Maybe a serious incident like a dirty bomb going off is just what the public needs to wake up to the lack of responsibility and leadership at the highest levels of this country. "Why do I have to do anything?" he asked out loud.

Luke watched a beetle moving through the dirt in the clearing. He picked up a stick and followed it, making a trail behind. It was a game Granddad had taught him when he was a young boy. Luke let his trail follow the beetle's path as it looped and circled over leaves, around pine cones, in and out of hoof prints, scurrying here and there in its own complex world. In a few seconds, the beetle stopped, and the trail ended—at his own boots.

His own boots. Luke closed his eyes. A parade of faces marched by: Marina and his daughters, waving from a blanket at Zuma Beach; his parents proudly saluting him when he marched in uniform one year in a Memorial Day parade; agents and analysts bent over their desks at the Bureau; Gennady and Vlada at the hospital, looking at him with pleading eyes; and finally, the strong, gentle face of his grandfather, nodding at him. Granddad had never offered much verbal praise, but when Luke built a fire the right way, or hit a target cleanly with a bow and arrow or tomahawk, or did anything correctly, he'd get the smile and the nod. That nod had meant more to Luke than any amount of verbal praise. Such a small movement produced so much power.

Granddad. How Luke missed him. He'd been taken away from Luke and the rest of his family too early, violently. It had been a cold, windy week in the north Wisconsin woods, but still, he and Granddad had had a good time camping. They were on their way home and stopped for gas outside a small, dumpy town.

◦   ◦   ◦

"Hope they've got gas," said Granddad. "Looks like not much else happens here. I'll do the pumping while you hit the bathroom."

"Okay," said Luke. He retrieved a key from the clerk and found the men's room around the back of the station.

He was washing his hands when he heard two gun shots, then the screech of tires. Luke's head jerked up from the sink. "Granddad?"

He ran to the front of the station. "Granddad!"

The clerk was already dead. Granddad had been shot at close range.

Luke grabbed a couple of rags and pressed them against his grandfather's chest.

"I'll get help, Granddad. Hang on."

His grandfather shook his head and reached for Luke's hand. He squeezed it once, tightly. And then, his eyes closed.

＊　　＊　　＊

THE PERPETRATOR had never been found. The station clerk and Luke's grandfather had been at the wrong place at the wrong time, victims of a random robbery.

Luke had despised guns since. In the Marine Corps and Bureau he had learned to use them efficiently but had prayed he'd never have to.

For years he'd blamed himself for his grandfather's death. If only he had left the washroom a minute earlier, he might have been able to help. Distract the robber. Something. Granddad hadn't spoken to Luke before he died, but Luke often remembered the peaceful look on his face. That face appeared before Luke again.

"Shit," he grunted, flicking the beetle away with the stick. He stood up and shouldered his pack. At the very least, he could ask some questions. Surely a few questions wouldn't steal his soul. His brain automatically began to make lists of people to contact.

At Route 40, he stuck out his thumb. It was a busy road and in a few minutes he was at the memorial.

He pulled his cell phone from his pack. He had a good signal and punched in a number at the Los Angeles FBI building.

"Charlie Logan."

"Hey, Charlie, it's me, Luke."

"Luke? Luke Chamberlin?"

"The one and only, Charlie."

"Where the hell are you, buddy?"

"Near Donner Pass. Look, something's come up. I need your help. I need to talk to you in person, though. Can you re-supply me anywhere north of here? I can wait if necessary. It's urgent, Charlie. I wouldn't ask otherwise."

"Jesus, Luke," replied Charlie, alarmed at the tone of Luke's voice. "I know you wouldn't."

Charlie thought for a few seconds. "Peg and Matt are going up to Sacramento next weekend to visit the grandparents. I could go along and then try to meet you. Is that soon enough?"

"Perfect," said Luke. "How about meeting me at Belden? You take Highway 70 out of Sacramento. Say, Saturday afternoon?"

"Yeah, I guess so, Luke." There was silence for a few moments between them. When Charlie spoke again, it was in a slow deliberate voice. "Remember what I said before you left the Bureau, Luke? Remember I told you to be satisfied with what you've accomplished and let go. Take the best, leave the rest. Remember?"

"Yeah, I know what you said, Charlie," Luke replied. "You'll need to stop by my house to pick up the supply box," he continued. "Marina will be mailing it in another few days."

Charlie sighed. "I can do that, Luke." Evidently Luke wasn't taking his advice.

"I've been through Belden. I'll meet you at the post office next Saturday afternoon. If there's a problem, I'll call you."

"See you soon, Charlie—and thanks." More cars drove into the lot. It would be a crowded and hot afternoon at the memorial, and the cool Donner Lake was inviting. But Luke had stopped contemplating the Donner Party or swimming.

He started thinking about people who could find out information and give him and Charlie some answers, the right answers, and dispense with any notion of dirty bombs exploding somewhere in the United States. A ridiculous notion, really.

He headed for the visitor's center to refill his water bottles and camel pack.

THIRTEEN

A THREE-YEAR-OLD FIRE had turned the land around the small pass in the northern Cascade Mountains into a charcoal pit. Here and there sprouts of green shoved up through the ash. A few trees had been spared, but most remained charred sentinels of the forest fire that had burned thousands of acres of the Okanogan-Wenatchee National Forest.

A small Forest Service guardhouse stood at the pass. At 6,200 feet, the only access to the house and surrounding area, besides foot or helicopter, was a steep dirt road with deadly drop-offs and no guard rails. This road wound down the mountain to a highway, which led to Mazama, a small town 15 miles away.

At the turn of the 19th century, copper, silver, zinc, and lead mines dotted the area. A bustling town built up around the boom. But the Klondike gold rush had lured miners farther north, and the mines near Harts Pass were abandoned. PCT hikers often hurried through. The area felt lifeless and still smelled of ruin.

Not to Mary Lou Jones, an intern ranger with the Forest Service at the Harts Pass station. Her primary job was to report smoke, but she also collected camping fees, explained to visitors what flora and fauna lived in the area, and helped the occasional stranded hiker or traveler with car troubles. This was her second summer as an intern, and she hoped her efforts would turn into a full-time job as a forest ranger.

She didn't mind the isolation. It was a welcome change from Phoenix, where she lived during the winter doing temp work as a data entry specialist. Each spring she couldn't wait to leave her small boxy house in a development full of small boxy houses only a few feet apart. At 25, she was ready for a solid career and nothing appealed to her more than being outdoors. Besides, civilization wasn't far. She had daily radio contact with the Forest Service in Mazama. And with satellite TV, the Internet, plenty of books, knitting, and her cat, Pinot, she was content.

Every day, Mary Lou was up by 6 A.M., washed and changed into her forest ranger uniform by 6:30, and ready to face whatever the day brought. Still, she was surprised to hear a truck rumble up the dirt road at 7. She turned the TV off and put on her official campaign hat, tucking her brown hair behind her ears. She straightened her sturdy frame and walked outside the guardhouse to greet the motorists. She looked out from under the wide brim of the felt hat.

"Morning. Can I help you?" she asked the three men and one woman who had stepped out of the beat-up Ford truck. They were casually dressed in blue jeans and T-shirts. Two of the men were bearded and dark-skinned, from the Middle East, Mary Lou guessed. They didn't say anything.

"Yes," replied the third, a clean-shaven westerner whose arm draped across the shoulders of a tall, angular woman. "We're looking for the hawks, the ones that migrate through here."

"Oh, you're too early," said Mary Lou. "It'll be another six weeks before they swing this way. If you go online, you can find out from the Forest Service website or the Audubon Society's Mazama Chapter exactly when they'll fly through."

Mary Lou was nothing if not thorough. "Pick a clear day to come back, with winds from the west or southwest, and bring binoculars with a wide field of view. On the right day, you'll see kestrels, red-tails, Cooper's and sharp-shinned hawks, osprey, and even golden eagles. There's nothing like it."

She pointed toward a rugged peak in the distance. "One of the best places to view the hawks is Slate Peak. It's about a three-mile walk from this station. Along the way, you can truly experience land above the tree line. We have unique species of trees and wildflowers that only grow up here. They've started to come back from the fire already."

One of the Middle Easterners took binoculars from a bag slung over his shoulder and scanned the land. He looked in the direction of her hand, toward Slate Peak, but then swung the binoculars farther to the left, to a campsite about a quarter mile away. It was empty and surrounded by shrubs and stumps of burned trees, as well as some new growth.

Just enough cover, the man thought, *yet not attractive to campers. Perfect for meeting our brothers.* He nodded in response to Mary Lou's meandering explanation of old mines also near Slate Peak and moved the binoculars back to the area she described. Then he returned them to his bag.

The westerner thanked Mary Lou, and the four birdwatchers climbed back into the truck. Mary Lou watched them rumble back down the road. A small corner of her brain noted something unusual. Was it the binoculars? They had been of a very high quality and powerful. But a lot of birders carried them.

Then it came to her, what was so unusual. When the Middle Easterner returned his binoculars to the bag, she had spied a pair of goggles just inside. She'd seen a similar pair displayed at a fire fighting seminar she'd attended that spring in Phoenix. *Those are night vision goggles. What are ornithologists doing with night vision goggles?* As far as she knew, hawks didn't migrate at night. Maybe they knew more about hawks than she did. Still, something didn't seem right. She'd make sure to note it in her next report to Mazama.

She stooped to pat the black and white cat. "Let's get some breakfast."

FOURTEEN

THE TRAIL leading to Belden from Mt. Pleasant descended to a deep gorge. Luke faced a downhill of thirty-six switchbacks in 6,000 feet. He loosened the straps at the top of his pack to ease the pressure on his shoulders and place more weight on his hips. He hadn't counted on such bad conditions. Water had been scarce so he'd had to carry a lot. Weighed down by a heavy pack, the trail to the juncture had been slow going, weaving in and out of gullies, across slopes and saddles, and up steep hills. He didn't want to be late meeting Charlie. He took longer strides to increase his speed, but too fast a pace brought sharp pains to his knees.

Below 4,000 feet, he saw less fir and pine, and more deciduous trees—oak, maple, thimbleberry, and shrubs. With this type of cover, came hazards of six-foot-high poison oak shrubs, ticks, and rattlesnakes. What elevation favored rattlesnakes—was it 5,000 feet or 3,000 feet? He slowed his pace a bit. Now wasn't the time to meet a snake or fall into a patch of poison oak.

The trail finally leveled and Luke caught sight of a freight train stopped on tracks. That meant Belden wasn't far.

According to his guide, Belden was a town, a collection of trailers really, inhabited by part-hippies, part-bikers. Once a successful gold mining operation, the hills around Belden were now full of methamphetamine labs, so he'd heard from agents in San Francisco. But it had a post office for package pickup, a bar, a few cabins to rent, and a place to do a wash. It was the perfect pit stop for thru-hikers. The guide had heartily recommended it.

Luke looked at the train stretching eternally in both directions. It had to be two miles long. He didn't relish squeezing himself and his pack underneath the cars, but he didn't see any other way. Then he spotted a note taped to a stick stuck in the ground. It pointed to a gap between cars. Lucky for hikers, the engineer had separated the length of freight cars so hikers could cross the tracks without crawling under them. He hurried through the gap and walked into town, pausing in front of the only real building, the Belden Gorge Saloon, a frontier-style, two-story brick and wood structure. In one half, the saloon offered beer and the famous Belden Burger. In the other half, a bare-bones general store sold a few essentials, mostly catering to fishermen. He continued past a rickety motel and RV sites and followed a road across the Feather River to the Belden Post Office, a building about the size and look of an outhouse.

Charlie was waiting for him, clean-shaven and comfortable in his usual rolled-up shirt sleeves and khaki pants. He waved and saw that Charlie carried not only a re-supply box, but also a six-pack of Sam Adams, his favorite beer.

"You look like hell," Charlie said, standing up to greet Luke. "And your hair's long enough to braid."

Luke smiled and shook the outstretched hand. "Thanks."

He spotted an empty picnic table nearby. "Let's go over there," he said, taking off his pack.

Luke motioned to the re-supply box. "Thanks for the food box. Looks like you brought lunch too."

"It's all yours," Charlie answered. "You need it."

"Does Peg know you're here?" asked Luke, unwrapping a sandwich.

"No," replied Charlie, "I told her I was going for a hike—which I am, sort of. I told her our walks around the Santa Monica Mountains inspired me."

He pulled a small handheld GPS receiver from his pocket. "Plus, I wanted to try out my new GPS, which she and Matt gave me for my birthday."

He tucked the receiver back into his pocket.

"Marina's been e-mailing around parts of your journal. I'm impressed, man. What a trip. Aren't you almost halfway there?"

"Yeah," replied Luke. "And it can't come soon enough. My knees are starting to wear down. Hikers are dropping like flies, according to the logs I've read at post offices along the way. They're either worn down physically, or mentally. It's too far for some people, or they lose their hiking buddies and can't go on solo."

Luke popped the top off a couple of beers. He handed one to Charlie and tipped his into his mouth. The ice-cold liquid slid down his throat. "Thanks, Charlie. This hits the spot."

"Thought it might."

"How's Marina doing?" Luke asked.

Charlie sipped his beer. "She's okay," he replied, "but the last time Peg talked to her, at our barbecue, she seemed frustrated, a little angry. I guess she doesn't like you being gone so long."

"I don't think she's angry about the hike, Charlie. She's upset because I don't have an important job lined up after I'm done. It's not like I don't have a pension or anything. I know she wants a nicer lifestyle, but I can't give it to her right now."

"This retirement process is a change for the whole family, not just you, Luke," said Charlie. "Give her some time, too."

Luke asked about Charlie's family, but ended the small talk quickly.

"Look," he said, "I need you to check on some things."

Charlie fell silent. He looked directly at Luke. "Sure," he replied. "But I hope it's not remotely related to anything you've done in the past 20 years, Luke."

"Remember that Soviet spy, Gennady Zukov? The one I uncovered?"

"Yeah, I remember," said Charlie. He chuckled. "I couldn't believe you two got to be friends. Spy vs. spy stuff."

"Gennady just contacted me. Through former spies, right here on the trail." Luke summarized the message he'd received from Gennady.

Charlie listened without comment. He hoped Luke wasn't getting paranoid, as some agents do after leaving the Bureau's bubble of isolation. But he saw no sign of anxiety or frenzy in Luke's face. Only the serious, intent face he'd always known.

"Maybe—and it's a big maybe—there's something going on," continued Luke. "Can you dig a little—let me know? I doubt there's anything there, but I don't remember Gennady being a big joker, and he went to a lot of trouble to get this message to me. Maybe even put himself in danger."

"What do you want to know for? Haven't you had enough?" asked Charlie.

"I have had enough," replied Luke, "but it won't hurt to do a little checking. Call it professional curiosity."

Charlie looked at Luke for a moment. It wasn't curiosity. It was Luke's hero complex, his insatiable urge to save the world. And there was nothing anyone could do to quell it.

"This isn't a good idea," said Charlie.

"Charlie, I have a hunch. Just ask a few questions, that's all."

"I'll see what I can do," Charlie said. He looked at his watch and stood up. "It's a long drive back to Sacramento. I'd better get going. You staying here the night?"

"Yeah, I got a motel room. Time for a shower and real bed."

"I'll call you," said Charlie.

Luke walked back into Belden and checked into the motel. He started a wash in the motel's laundry room and had a long shower. The steam and hot stream of water relaxed and unbent his muscles and bones. He hadn't recalled a shower feeling so good. As he toweled off, he pinched the flesh on his stomach. He'd lost a lot of his body fat getting through the Sierras, even with a couple of days off at Vermilion Ranch where he'd eaten nonstop. He hadn't had much extra fat to begin with. He was probably down to his high school weight. He worried that his body was starting to digest muscle for energy. By late morning each day on the trail, he felt weak and had to break for lunch sooner and sooner. He'd begun eating his dinner packs for lunch. With only half the trail done, that didn't bode well. He'd need to take an extra day or two off soon.

Luke finished dressing and opened the re-supply box to sort out what he needed for the next section. All the food was there: Pemmican bars; Mountain House dehydrated dinners; Pop-Tarts for quick energy; garlic paste to add taste to dinner and keep bugs away; trail mix; tubes of peanut butter; powdered soup mix for taste and salt; granola mixed with powdered coffee, cocoa, milk, and granular honey; powdered Gatorade; a big jar of ibuprofen and one of mega-vitamins; and tea. At the bottom of the box, he found a funny drawing from his girls, two silly faces saying "Go Dad Go!" and "Half Way There!" But there was no note from Marina.

As he cleaned out and re-organized his pack, he came across Sea Dog's phone number. He wondered where the ex-SEAL was. Luke plugged in his cell phone and dialed Mike's number.

Mike picked up on the second ring. "Hello?" Laughter and music in the background muffled his answer.

"Mike. It's Camper. I got your message at Echo Lake. Thanks. You must be burning up the trail. Where are you?"

"Luke!" answered Mike, "I'm in Belden, at the saloon. Where are you?"

Luke smiled. "Not far."

·　·　·

LUKE FOUND MIKE SITTING at a corner table at one end of the saloon. At the other end, a row of bikers dressed in wife-beater T-shirts, torn jeans, and leather boots slumped on stools at a long, plywood bar. A TV on the wall showed reruns of old baseball games. Country music blared from a juke box. Between the bar and group of tables, a few locals hit balls on a rickety pool table. They stared at Luke when he walked by.

"Didn't know if you'd catch up, Camper," said Mike, standing up to shake hands.

"Yeah, well I wondered that myself," replied Luke, grabbing a chair. They motioned for the waitress.

A thin, worn woman walked over. "What do you want." she said to Luke.

"Try the local Valley Ale," suggested Mike. "It's not bad."

"I'll have that, thanks," Luke said to the waitress.

"She doesn't seem too happy with her job," he added.

"No," said Mike, "the whole place sends off bad vibes. Those bikers probably just came in from a hard day's work at the meth labs. But the guide said the food was good. Let's order that burger. I'm starved."

When the waitress returned, they each ordered another beer, nachos and cheese for an appetizer, the soup of the day, and the Belden Burger.

Halfway through the soup, the bar grew quiet. The two men at the pool table had stopped playing and were eyeing a biker who'd gotten up from the bar and moved toward Luke and Mike. His head was shaved and the back of his T-shirt read: If you can read this, the bitch fell off.

"Hey, hiker trash," he slurred. "Time to walk. We got more friends coming and we need the room."

Mike looked around. "I see plenty of empty tables." He tipped the bowl of soup to his mouth, drank the rest, then placed the bowl on the table. "And we're not trash."

"Just ignore him. He's drunk," said Luke.

The biker took an unsteady step closer. "I said you was trash. Maybe we need to show you out to the dumpster."

He looked around for his buddies, guffawing at his own joke. Two more bikers rose from the bar.

"I really want to finish my dinner," said Luke.

"Doesn't look like we're going to," replied Mike. He put his napkin on the table. "I assume Granddad showed you how to fight?"

"He did, but it's been a while."

"What about the FBI?"

"Had to flip a female in a combat course once. Does that count?"

Mike grimaced. "Great."

"Look," said Mike, addressing the group. "We're tired. We just want to eat our dinner. Then we'll go."

"You're gonna go now!" The biker lurched toward Mike.

In a quick upper cut, Mike put his fist into the biker's face. The surprised well-wisher staggered backwards but stayed on his feet. Mike kicked the side of his knee to complete his fall to the floor. He didn't get up.

His two buddies near the bar pulled out knives.

Luke stepped to the pool table and grabbed a cue ball. One of the men fell to the floor unconscious. He never saw the cue ball flying at his jaw at 90 miles per hour. The other man came at Luke, jabbing his knife. Luke yanked a pool stick from one of the players. The biker's eyes were glazed, either from drugs or beer or both. He reeked. *Worse than the she bear*, Luke thought. He made a strong thrust, but Luke smoothly turned away and knocked the knife from the biker's hand with the pool stick. Another hit on the back, another to the groin, and he was down.

Mike was tossing a drunk local over his shoulder when the sound of a round being placed into a shotgun stopped the brawl.

"That's enough," said the saloon's proprietor, holding up the gun. "Everyone go home."

The patrons picked themselves up and stumbled out the door.

Luke and Mike asked to have the rest of their dinner boxed. At a picnic table behind the motel, they finished their meal.

Mike clinked his beer to Luke's and grinned. "Not bad work for a jarhead."

Luke shook his head. "Town's not too friendly."

"Yeah, but the burgers are great," said Mike.

FIFTEEN

LUKE STOPPED in front of a small granite post at the side of the trail, just south of Route 36. He slipped off his pack, pulled out a bottle of water and took a long drink. A day out of Belden, and he was feeling tired and dehydrated. The six-pack of beer he and Mike started had turned into another, and he'd gotten pretty wasted. But he'd needed a night like the one at the saloon. He and Mike made a decent team. The more time he spent with the ex-SEAL, the more he liked him. Most of the thru-hikers had left the trail at this point, or were considering it. Halfway to Canada, Mike was still strong and motivated. What else would you expect from a SEAL. A good guy to have on your side, if the need ever arose. Mike had stayed in Belden to wait for re-supplies and meet again with his sponsors, but Luke was sure he'd catch up in Oregon or early in Washington.

Luke had chosen to continue, though his knees had warned otherwise. At this point, the Sierras had given way to a new mountain range—the volcanic Cascades. He'd pass Lassen Peak soon, the first in a string of old volcanoes that stretched the rest of the way to Canada. Already the grey volcanic dust permeated his gators and socks and coated his feet in grit.

Although the guide described this section as badly eroded and overgrown in some places, the trail proved gentle, at least compared to the Sierras. He'd be able to put in 30-mile days even with sore knees. In Ashland, he'd take a few days to rest and fuel up.

Luke stared at the granite post. He pulled out his cell phone. He had a decent signal and dialed his home number.

Marina picked up, breathing heavily. "Hold on, Luke," she said, "I've got to get some water. I just walked in the door from a club run."

Luke heard her place the phone down and open the refrigerator where she always kept a pitcher full of cold water. She belonged to a local running club, which organized a run once a week along one of several routes into the local hills. He imagined exactly how she looked. Thick, black hair pulled back into a pony tail with a few wet strands pasted against her face; a patch of sweat showing through her tank top between her shoulder blades; her long, still-trim legs in running shorts. He remembered how those legs had attracted him in college.

*   *   *

"Marina. That's a pretty name." He was leaning against a doorway of the living room in the frat house. She was sitting on the edge of a stuffed chair, her legs extending from beneath a short skirt, smooth and bare except for a pair of sandals. Her dark skin and black hair were an unusual sight at the University of Wisconsin where fair-skinned northern European students were more the norm. He'd been instantly drawn to her.

"Thanks. It means 'of the sea.'" She shrugged and smiled. "I'm from New Mexico. No idea how I got the name."

She gestured to his hair, tied at the nape of his neck. "I'll bet you've got a name that comes with a story."

"Not really. Just Luke." He moved to sit beside her. She smelled of prairie grass, herbal, deep, and undiscovered. "My grandfather's a Chippewa. He'd like to see my hair in a braid. But my dad wants me to cut it short, like my brothers."

"What about your mother?"

"I'm not so sure about her. She's from the Chippewa side. She's kind of quiet, but I think she likes it this way."

He offered Marina a beer, and conversation about home and family, about her desire to be a nurse, and his to serve his country, passed easily between them.

After a few dates, it was clear they wanted to be with each other. They spent as much time as possible together.

᠗   ᠗   ᠗

LUKE GRADUATED two years ahead of Marina, and while he served with the Third Marine Division on Okinawa, Marina received her general nursing degree. After his obligation with the military was done, they married. Luke joined the FBI, and while he served at the Newark office, Carrie and Grace were born. Luke's long hours hadn't given Marina time to pursue her own dreams. Instead, she had concentrated on raising the girls. Working part time as a school nurse fit her schedule, and while it wasn't challenging, it was a flexible job that had moved whenever they did.

Marina came back on the line. Her voice was business-like. "How are you doing, Luke?"

"I'm good." He decided not to tell her about his weight loss. "All parts still intact. How is your run club going? Are you still at the front?"

"Sort of," she answered, her voice softening a bit. "I manage to stay up near the leaders, but I'll never keep pace with them. They're just too fast. I might start training for a 10-K in a few weeks."

"That's great."

"I made it to Charlie's barbecue," she added. "The girls talked me into going. You didn't miss anything, Luke, same people, same conversations. But it was nice to catch up with Charlie and Peg."

"I'm glad you went, Mari. They're good friends."

"Look, Mari," he continued, trying not to sound anxious, "I might not stay exactly on schedule. The dates to send my re-supply packages may change, but I'll let you know in plenty of time if they do."

"Why, Luke? I thought you were making good time."

Luke was careful in how he phrased his answer. "I am, but I'm helping Charlie with a situation. Doing a little checking around. Nothing that will take me off the trail."

There was a long pause on Marina's end of the line.

"Oh, now I get it," she snapped. "Now I know why Gennady called. He was trying to tell you something. And Charlie stopping by here for your re-supply box—he was going to meet you. And I thought he was being so kind to give it to you in person."

Luke heard the whack of a glass being slammed on the counter.

"Luke, don't get involved. This is the last thing you need. First you hate the Bureau and can't wait to retire. Now you're helping those bastards. You know they don't give a shit about you or what you've done. I don't understand, Luke. You'll never learn."

Luke was quiet. They'd had many conversations about his dedication to the Bureau. Work hours that were too long. His compulsion to do what was right.

"How are Carrie and Grace, Marina?"

Marina sighed. "They're fine. They made it to the finals in doubles at the Ventura Junior Tournament. Gracie seems to like her job at the movie theater—but you know Gracie. It's hard to tell."

"Are they around?" asked Luke. He'd have to hang up soon to save power.

"No, they went to the pool with friends."

"Tell them I liked their notes."

The cell phone signal faded and returned.

"I'm losing you, Marina," said Luke, "but I wanted to tell you. I called to tell you. This spot where I'm standing, it's halfway, halfway to Canada!"

"That's great," replied Marina. "Maybe you should keep right on going once you get there. Seems like you don't want to be here anymore, and there are a lot of woods in Canada to build a cabin."

Luke was shocked at her words. "Marina," he said, "that's not true. I…"

"Luke," interrupted Marina. "Finish your damn hike." She hung up.

Luke clicked the cell phone off. He took a deep breath. Marina had never spoken so harshly. Was she overwhelmed with handling the twins? Or was she really fed up with his nonchalant attitude about their future and her life as a smiling, supporting wife?

Luke put on his pack. Red fir trees lined each side of the trail. The deeply grooved bark was a chocolate color that glinted red in the sun. It felt rough and thick, impermeable to the intrusion of anything, even fire. The massive column-like trunks reminded Luke of the tall Eastern white pines that grew in northern Wisconsin. Granddad used to pick the young cones and stew them up with rabbit.

He bent to touch the giant fir cones lying on the path next to the stone post. They were arranged in a number: 1,325. One thousand, three hundred, and twenty five miles. Halfway. He should have felt excited, but he didn't.

SIXTEEN

MAHMOUD STEPPED from the banca onto Dalahican Beach and grabbed the outrigger of the long, dugout fishing boat to steady himself. Three weeks on and off fishing boats had left his legs rubbery. Although it was only 4 A.M. and still dark, the air was warm and humid. The fish market near the beach was already lit. Small fishing boats, like the banca that carried Mahmoud to shore, continued to land along this quiet stretch of Tayabas Bay. Dressed in jeans, a T-shirt, and straw hat, Mahmoud looked like the other fishermen unloading their catch.

It had been a long and trying journey from Karachi to the Philippines, but Allah's soldiers had organized his trip well. Before he left Karachi, he was given western clothes and a backpack. A small box wrapped in newspaper and tied with string lay at the bottom of the pack. "You are to take this music box to Vancouver," he had been told. "Guard it with your life." For a music box, it was very heavy, but he had not asked any questions. He did not need to. It was enough of an honor to be chosen for something so important to the cause. He had, instead, placed his toiletries, a few clothes, and his Koran on top.

Mahmoud had started his journey from Karachi to the Philippines in fairly large vessels, mostly trawlers that dragged for tuna in the Arabian Sea. He stayed on one trawler for a few days as it fished. When it returned to port, he switched to another. The boats always returned to small ports—first along the west coast of India, past Sri Lanka, through the Strait of Malacca, into the South China Sea, and across to the Philippines. He never stayed on land for more than a day, usually less. Then it was back out to sea.

Mahmoud had spent the first week in a bunk seasick beyond his imagination. The crew offered little help beyond crackers and a bit of broth. He couldn't eat. He couldn't pray. In a bad storm on the Arabian Sea, he truly believed he would die. Even Allah couldn't ease his fear of the unrelenting waves that swept across the ship's deck. He thought of home, his mother's patient voice, his sister's laugh, his dog's hopeful look at a bit of extra meat. And his neatly made cot in his small, still room.

Even when the sickness abated, he was afraid to leave his bunk. The ocean was as foreign to Mahmoud as the moon. The endless water and the endless sound of it tossing the boat. The walls of waves. The fish. Not just tuna, but bulky sharks, wide stingrays, and skates. After a couple of weeks, he learned to live on the sea, to move with the waves, not against them. And to not fear the fish as they flopped on the deck. He had helped haul nets. He found he liked the smell of the salt air. On calm days, he watched dolphins and flying fish surface and dive off the ship's bow wake. Even so, he had looked forward to touching land. Each time he changed boats, he kneeled and kissed the earth. He prayed to Allah to give him strength and found enough to board the next boat. Each time it had grown easier, even when he was transferred to smaller and smaller boats.

Mahmoud had climbed into the banca at a bamboo raft anchored in the middle of the bay at 1 A.M. From the raft, a man fished with a hand line. Mahmoud waited until he had filled the banca with sardines and sat quietly in the bow while he paddled the half mile to shore.

When they reached the beach, the fisherman nodded toward the market. Mahmoud took his backpack from the boat and walked to the entrance. He listened to the whispers of the fish brokers bidding on the anchovies, goatfish, roundscads, and tuna. So far, the men helping him had been efficient and on time, and Mahmoud knew he'd soon be met.

SEVENTEEN

TERRI HAD JUST SAT DOWN at her desk when the phone rang. "Hey Terri. Charlie Logan. Had your coffee yet?"

Terri smiled. Only one other person got to work as early as she did. Charlie. When she first arrived, he'd gone out of his way to help her and had treated her like a professional. She had grown to trust him, especially now that Luke was gone.

"On the second cup, Charlie. And thanks again for asking me to your barbecue. It was fun. You've got some nice neighbors."

"Yeah, they're good folks," replied Charlie. "Say, Terri, if you've got a minute, I'd like to come by. I've got a couple of questions."

"Sure, Charlie, I'm the only one here."

Terri wondered what was up. Although the really good managers like Charlie walked around the floors now and then to say hello and make themselves available for concerns, it wasn't common practice to meet in an analyst's pod.

Charlie arrived with his own coffee. He took the extra chair near Terri's desk. "I've been going over some of our recent investigations into terrorist activities," he said, "the ones

111

you mentioned to me at the party. I wondered if you could clarify a few things."

"I'll try to," replied Terri. She considered why Charlie was asking her rather than Dirk Barnstable. All of her reports had gone up to the counterterrorism squad supervisor. Then she remembered Dirk's IQ.

"I see that some of the increased chatter documented in your reports—the meetings, phone conversations—is from the Philippines. Even though the Philippine army has reduced numbers of terrorist cells in recent years, we know they still operate in parts of that country."

"Yes," agreed Terri, "we continue to help them by sending down Special Forces to train their military, and I believe our joint programs to fight terrorism there are having some success."

"You also discussed the movement of something across Pakistan," said Charlie.

It was clear to Terri that Charlie had read her latest report carefully. She felt pleased, and also relieved that someone else seemed concerned.

"Can you elaborate on this? Got anything else on the scope?" he asked.

"As a matter of fact, yes," answered Terri. "I just sent a memo up to Dirk yesterday. The Canadian Secret Intelligence Service has reported that some sort of 'event' may soon take place, possibly in Vancouver. Something about a package or perhaps a person. They weren't specific. Or they won't yet say."

Terri thought she saw Charlie take a short, sharp breath. She continued. "I flagged the message but haven't heard back from Dirk about wanting more information."

Charlie looked intently at her. "Vancouver?"

Terri nodded. "Things have happened there before. That case in 2000, when the would-be millennium bomber took a ferry from Victoria through the San Juan Islands. Supposedly, he was heading to LAX to blow it up New Year's Eve. Lucky for the customs agents, he was sweating bullets."

"Yes, I remember." Charlie's jaw muscle tightened. "But what does this have to do with Pakistan?"

Terri leaned forward. "I see trends in the data, Charlie. Something, or somebody important, is coming over here, maybe across the Pacific. As you know, Pakistan's port, Karachi, is a gateway to the Arabian Sea. It's not a stretch to reach the Philippines via boat from there. And lots of tankers leave Subic Bay for Canada. It's become one of the biggest ports in the world. Every piece of intel points to something, or someone, coming across the Pacific. Charlie, I'm worried."

When Terri first arrived, it hadn't taken long for Charlie to see that she was unusual in both her intelligence and willingness to work hard. He trusted not only her analyses, but her instincts.

"I agree," he said, standing up. "Let's pay a visit to Dirk."

*   *   *

"YEAH, I SAW THE REPORT," drawled Dirk in his Texas accent, looking from one to the other. "I was about to forward it upstairs, but they're deluged with this stuff."

"This is urgent," said Charlie. "Forget forwarding the message. Let's go see Bill."

"Okay," replied Dirk, getting up from his chair, "But you know Bill."

"Cute suit," Dirk said casually to Terri as they walked out his door. Terri glared back.

Bill Scully, the assistant special agent in charge of the counterterrorism program, surveyed the three of them standing in front of his desk. A former Ivy League football star, his walls were covered with his team's memorabilia. He hadn't made it as a lawyer in the private sector, so he joined the Bureau where his hours were a little more nine-to-five. He'd transferred from Headquarters six months ago.

Bill knew Robert Mayberry, the current director of the FBI, who also had been a football-playing Ivy Leaguer. He had sensed rapid advancement and wanted to play his cards just right. He took his time addressing them, propping his expensive-looking shoes on his desk. The holes in the bottoms of them prompted Terri to cough in order to stifle a laugh. *Guess his government salary doesn't keep him dressed the way he was accustomed to.*

"Well, the three musketeers, is it?" Bill asked. "What can I do for you?"

Terri bristled at the condescending remark, but Charlie didn't waste any time. "Bill, we've got good intel telling us about a possible dirty bomb coming our way, maybe through Vancouver."

Charlie saw he at least had Bill's attention. He made his case.

"Borders between our countries are notoriously unmonitored, and trails and dirt-road crossings are everywhere. Canada has a very lax immigration and asylum program, and Vancouver has little security in place. Terrorists have tried it once before—remember the millennium bomber in 2000. They may be focused on trying again. And again. Until they succeed. Just like the Twin Towers. "

Terri and Dirk stared open-mouthed at Charlie. Terri's reports hadn't specifically indicated a dirty bomb. *Charlie must have other information,* Terri thought. *Where did it come from?*

"At least, let's put some increased manpower on it," continued Charlie, ignoring their stares. "I'd like to involve more resources from the JTTF's local sources in Oregon and Washington."

Bill removed his feet from the desk and sat straight in his chair. "Whoa, whoa, guys. We've heard all of this before. Every day. I'm not taking it any further until you get more specifics. We don't want to bother Jen with this unless we're absolutely sure. Besides, she's gone for the week—a management retreat in Santa Barbara for the top dogs."

He shuffled papers on his desk. "Come back when you've got more."

Out in the hallway, Dirk nudged Charlie. "Told you. Jen's playing a lot of golf these days. Hard to imagine that swinging a club past those breasts is easier than making a decision, but it must be so. See you guys." He winked at Terri. "Keep me in the loop."

Charlie turned to Terri. "He's not bothering you, is he?"

"No," she replied. "I've made it quite clear that I'm not interested."

They walked toward the elevator. "Let me know if he does," said Charlie, "and stay on this. I don't have a good feeling. Copy me on all of your intel and get help from other analysts if you need to. Good job."

"Okay, Charlie," responded Terri, "but, how did you conclude there might be a dirty bomb? I didn't include anything about that possibility in my reports." Even as she asked the question, she knew she probably wouldn't get an answer from the JTTF supervisor.

"A good source," Charlie only said. He hurried to his office and closed the door. He considered the string of terrorist attacks since 9/11—London, Barcelona, Bali. *The United States had, at first, reacted with anger, beefed up security, created a new agency to protect the country, sent troops to war—but they hadn't stayed vigilant. Life went on as it did in the rest of the world. What the hell—why not another attack?*

Charlie began to piece together an unnerving puzzle: information from Luke indicated dirty material sold in Russia; then movement of something across Pakistan—a dirty bomb? Charlie had read several reports on Central Asia. This area of "stans" formed yet another front for fighting terrorists, with rebels, jihadists, freedom fighters—whatever they liked to call themselves—emerging daily. And while many of the "stans" backed the U.S.-led fight against terrorism, there were well-funded factions that did not. Plus, five of the countries were former Soviet republics. Maybe Moscow was putting political pressure on some of them.

Terri's information showed increased meetings and telephone conversations in the Philippines; now, friendly intelligence showed something going on in Vancouver. *Christ, Luke's intel is right! Terrorists could be planning an attack, probably through a clandestine cell system that stretches from Central Asia through the Philippines, across to Vancouver, and then down the west coast of the U.S.*

Charlie considered his options. Help definitely wouldn't come from the FBI. They were too slow to react. Nor, probably, from his task force, which, while able and ready, was consistently wrapped up in red tape and internal office quarrels. Lately, more time had been spent on internal power plays than on counterterrorism. No, he needed to go outside for this. But, go outside the Bureau? It could end his career. He tilted his head back and stared at the ceiling. He thought about his recent promotion to head of the JTTF. With 10 years left before retirement, he was in a good place in the career advancement program. He thought about his family and their security, their future. All of that could change with a phone call. But doing nothing was worse.

He picked up the phone and punched the phone number of Leon Malone. Not only was Leon a former member of the JTTF, he also was fond of Luke. On first meeting, Charlie recalled, Leon had recognized dedication and loyalty in Luke, and had immediately trusted him. He'd believe the intel if he knew Luke was involved.

"Leo?" Charlie said, when Leon picked up.

"Hey, Charles," replied Leon, "you haven't called to fish lately. What's up?"

"Plenty," replied Charlie. "Got a minute? I need you to make a few calls for me."

"I'm all ears."

Charlie told Leon about his meeting with Luke and the failure to generate any interest or reaction from management.

"Christ almighty! The end of the world, of California anyway, and this is the response you get. How did I know that?"

Leon's reaction was what Charlie had expected. He held the phone away from his ear while Leon raged.

"I don't think my team can respond fast enough," explained Charlie, "even to do some checking. Luke will be in Oregon soon and could use some help poking around. I know I'm way out on a limb here."

"Yeah, you are. You could get shit-canned for this, Charles."

"I'm aware of that."

Leon remained silent.

Charlie waited.

"I might know of a few local guys who can find what's going on," said Leon. "Leave it to me."

Leon hit the off button on his phone. In his years as a detective and member of the JTTF, he had investigated everything from murders to robberies and gang violence. But nothing with potential ramifications like this. If a dirty bomb—or bombs—went off in San Francisco or L.A., sections of the cities would be unlivable for months.

And there was Luke, in the middle of it. Luke, the steadfast tin soldier.

He turned on his cell phone and started making calls.

EIGHTEEN

THE TRAIL THROUGH OREGON had, in parts, been stunning, especially the areas around Crater Lake and Mt. Hood. The guide had been right. In southern Oregon, steep elevations and dramatic views had been the exception, rather than the norm. But now, Luke hurried, paying little attention to the scenery. He looked forward to getting past Mt. Jefferson and down to Cascade Locks where he'd resupply and perhaps find an update from Charlie.

He'd had a good rest in Ashland—three days of doing nothing but eating good food, relaxing, and watching TV. His knees felt reborn.

He hadn't seen anything about terrorists on the television or in newspapers while he was off the trail. Domestic issues had focused on wildfires in the West and droughts in the East. Several hours spent at an Internet café in town, searching for information on recent international terrorist attacks or attempted transport of hazardous material out of Russia, or another country, brought up nothing. Nada for blogs and tweets. He'd read about some unrest in Thailand and Africa,

119

and demonstrations in Tibet and Kyrgyzstan, but nothing that pointed to an immediate threat to the West.

A phone conversation with Charlie, his second day in Ashland, suggested otherwise. Terri had done a good job sorting out the intel, and Charlie had put together a scenario that had pointed to the possible movement of dirty bomb material into Vancouver. Thank God there were a few people left in the L.A. office with some thinking skills and foresight. Whatever was happening, though, was staying out of the news. Charlie said he'd contacted Leon. Good. There was a guy who could find out what, if anything, was going on.

During his three days off the trail, he'd also had a good talk with Grace and Carrie. He'd needed to hear them laugh and tease him. He smiled when he recalled their yucks and ughs at the thought of how he looked with a beard and 30 pounds lighter.

"That's disgusting," said Grace with not a little disdain in her voice. "Doesn't food get stuck in your beard?"

"Eewww, Dad, I bet you look like a Sasquatch," piped in Carrie. "They've been seen up there. They might mistake you for one."

They both burst into giggles.

"It's not that bad, girls," said Luke, but he laughed, too.

Marina hadn't been home. He'd left his motel room number, but she hadn't called back. She seemed fine, the girls had said, but what did two busy teenagers know about how their mother really felt?

He looked at the trail ahead. Compared to the Sierras, Oregon's eroded volcanic peaks seem stunted, and the lunar-like trail almost easy to traverse. His motions across the old, black lava fields were smooth and light. But with 600 miles left to the border, he knew his elation was only temporary. He still had a long way to go, undoubtedly with some difficult conditions to negotiate.

This part of the PCT was well-traveled. Prints from countless travelers, both long-distance and day hikers, had left impressions in the dirt, crisscrossed with those of animals. He glanced at two rows of tracks. A couple. The deep imprints indicated a heavy hiker, or one carrying a big pack, likely the male. Parallel to those prints were lighter, narrower tracks and more of them. The female. The fine, sharp edges of the prints indicated they weren't too far ahead. Marmot tracks dotting the tops of shallower boot prints told of day-walkers who had passed much earlier. *What a mix of lives walks here.*

Luke reflected on the 100 or so thru-hikers who remained on the PCT and the 200 others who had started, but had not made it this far, their dreams not yet achieved. With only a few hundred miles left, his goal felt within reach. He hoped Charlie had any security situation under control.

A feather on the trail caught Luke's attention. He bent over to pick it up. It was about six inches long and completely black, until he looked closely and saw the colors of a rainbow in it. A crow's feather. Marina would say such a find was good luck. Crows were one of her favorite birds. When they were little, the girls loved to hear their mother tell the story of how Crow came to be black and have a hoarse voice. He remembered the story well. Crow, once a brightly colored bird with a beautiful voice, had volunteered to fly to the Sky God and ask for fire to warm the earth, which was buried in snow. On the way back to earth, soot from the burning faggot Crow held in his mouth turned his feathers black and his voice hoarse. Crow thought he was disgraced among birds, until the Sky God reminded him that never would man want to hunt him for his feathers or cage him for his song. Crow would always be free. Luke liked that ending. He ran the smooth feather across his cheek and tucked it into his pack. Marina. Did he want to be free from her?

His thoughts returned to Charlie. More questions. What if there was something in Vancouver? What if the JTTF couldn't handle it? What if the Canadian Secret Intelligence Service missed connections? A dirty bomb exploding would make one hell of a mess. That thought deeply disturbed him. Well, he'd done his job. He'd contacted all the right people. They could take it from here.

Mt. Jefferson loomed closer. It was a spectacular peak, with a pointy tip and steep sides skirted in glaciers. Sweeps of alpine grasses and flowers covered the lower slopes.

The stunning view didn't last long. Clouds were beginning to gather around Jefferson's gnarly peak. Typical, he knew, of this elevation. Clear one minute, cloudy the next. He picked up his pace. He needed to reach a decent place to camp below tree line, in case the weather deteriorated. The last place he wanted to be was exposed to wind and lightning.

A juncture stopped his progress. The main trail seemed to turn right, another veered left. He pulled out his map, which indicated that the main trail continued straight and slightly uphill, even though it was narrow and not well-kept. Luke looked right. *Maps aren't perfect. Maybe the trail dips down then back up.* He took it.

After nearly an hour of constant downhill, he knew he'd gone wrong. He turned around and headed back up, feeling a chilly breeze against his face. He could smell the rain coming.

"Hi," a voice startled him. A tall, lean woman with sandy hair that hung loosely around her face was moving fast down the trail. By the looks of her equipment, she was an experienced hiker. "This the PCT? The juncture back there wasn't too clear."

"I thought it was," replied Luke, "but it just leads downhill, probably eventually to a trail head. I think the main trail is back at the juncture."

She pulled out her map. "Funny, the map says this way."

"Yeah, that's what I thought, but I've just walked a quarter mile back up. There's nothing down there but more down."

She hesitated. "I hope you're right."

She turned to follow Luke. "You look like a thru-hiker."

"I'm Luke, er, Camper," he said, pointing to his pack. "It must not be too hard to tell the thru-hikers at this point."

"I'm Naomi. No trail name. I'm section hiking Oregon and maybe some of Washington. I did parts of California the past two summers."

Naomi easily matched Luke's stride, even uphill.

Luke slowed his pace. "I've seen you somewhere," he said. "Were you at Links Internet Café in Ashland a couple days ago?"

Naomi studied Luke for a moment. "Yes, I was. I don't remember seeing you."

"You were pretty focused on what you were typing."

"Well, I guess I was trying to get a lot of emails out before I got back on the trail."

"Sounds like you hike a lot," Luke said.

"I do. Whenever I can get away. I'm a hospice nurse in Portland, and I get burned out pretty fast."

"That's a tough job."

"It can be. The mountains help. I need them. How about you? What's your story?"

Luke looked up. Clouds smudged the sky in gray piles. "Oh, I've just retired from a career in law enforcement. This trip is a retirement gift to myself."

"Law enforcement." Naomi repeated the words softly, slowly. "Talk about tough."

"Sometimes." He picked up his pace. " I don't like the looks of that sky. We've got to get back to the trail and then below tree line. I don't want to be in the open if the sky lets loose."

Lightning lit the sky. It began to rain. Then it poured.

"Too late," Naomi said.

"Jesus. We'll get soaked if we keep going." Luke peered through the sheets of rain. "There's a gully over there next to some boulders. Come on."

Naomi nodded, already starting to shiver. Luke threw up his tent. They dove into it, gear and all. They shoved their packs to each end of the tent, making a small space to sit. It was cramped, but warm.

"I should have known this was the wrong trail," said Luke. "I was in too much of a hurry."

"I don't think we're far off," replied Naomi. "Besides, I'm glad I ran into you. Who knows where I'd be now."

She offered Luke some jerky and trail mix.

"Yeah, well, we won't be too comfortable, but at least we're warm. I've got Pemmican bars. I see jerky is a favorite of yours."

Luke and Naomi talked into the night. They learned they had much in common, from a love of mountains to politics. Luke told her about Marina and the girls, and growing up in the wilds of Wisconsin under his grandfather's care. Naomi told Luke about her job.

"Why hospice nursing?" Luke asked.

"My mother was a hospice patient," Naomi replied. "Neither of us knew what to expect. The hospice nurse explained each step my mother was going through, and it made the experience much less frightening for both of us. Since I was already a nurse, I felt I could do the same for other families."

She chewed on the last of her Pemmican bar. "I get something out of it, too, something more than just feeling like I'm doing a good thing. I've grown more aware of life, of living it."

Naomi also told Luke about her ex-husband. "No children," she said. "We didn't have time before he cheated on me."

Their eyes locked and Luke's heart lurched in a way he hadn't felt for a while. Naomi looked away.

"I'm tired, Luke," she broke the moment. But she grinned. "Let's hope your tent holds up." She turned her back to him and nestled into her sleeping bag.

For a long time Luke listened to the rain pelting the tent and Naomi's steady breathing. He watched the sleeping bag lift and fall as she breathed. He laid a hand on the sleeping bag, but withdrew it when she twitched. He turned his head and felt something brush his cheek—the crow feather. Luke held it tightly and fell asleep.

Luke and Naomi woke to a clear sky. Luke pulled out his map and saw they weren't very far off the trail. He cursed himself again for his stupidity in not knowing exactly where they were yesterday.

If the sky had cleared overnight, Luke's feelings for Naomi had not. He wondered how she felt. Sharing the same tent hadn't produced any awkwardness in her. She was cheerful and talkative as she crawled out of the tent into the cool, early light. She poured her granola into a bowl then poked at his plain oat mixture. "Here," she said, spooning some of her granola into his bowl. "It's got figs and coconut and dried cherries in it. Live a little, Luke."

There was no question about hiking together as they headed for Cascade Locks.

NINETEEN

NEAR PIER 3, Mahmoud watched the men handle the cranes that loaded containers on the merchant ship. It was late in the day, and they hurried to finish before the sun set. In another few minutes, he'd board the huge ship, posing as a deck hand. The ship was bound for Canada, he'd been told, and that someone would show him what to do.

Mahmoud scanned the waterfront, a coagulum of buildings, wharves, ships, and machines that creaked and banged and hissed. Piers jutted into the harbor like long, bony arms. Cranes grew like crooked trees. Mountainous ships blotted the sky from his view.

Subic Bay's dozen container terminals extended westward into the bay. To the southwest, the bay narrowed, then opened to the South China Sea, and beyond that, the Philippine Sea, and then the immense Pacific Ocean. Mahmoud's stomach churned when he considered the long journey ahead, but he had survived the weeks before on much smaller boats. He'd survive this.

He thought about his family, squatting in a shack among the dry hills and goats. What time of day was it there? Was his father milking? Was his mother making a meal of curried rice and vegetables? Maybe there would be potatoes.

He remembered his mother saying no to his plans, her stricken face, when he had turned away. His father's disappointment. He loved them, but wished they had understood the meaning of the lessons at his madrassa. No matter how often he had tried to explain, they would not accept it. They would not even listen. His headmaster once repeated a section of text in Hadith, a body of Muslim scripture separate from the Koran. "If you memorize the Koran," the saying went, "you can take 10 other people with you to heaven and your parents will be crowned in heaven and given special status." That is what he wanted, for his parents to be crowned in heaven.

He breathed in the warm ocean air. He'd already nearly memorized the Koran. *This mission will bring crowns to them all.*

The last of the 20-foot-long containers was fastened to the ship's deck. Mahmoud wondered what was in them. *Boxes full of items to satisfy Western materialism, no doubt. It is just as my teachers said.* He still hadn't opened the package that rested at the bottom of his backpack, though he knew it wasn't a music box. He was certain it had something to do with bringing justice for Islamic people everywhere. That was enough for him. He fingered his backpack. *I have something for the West, too. Glory for Allah.*

"We are ready," a voice said to Mahmoud's right. Mahmoud nodded and followed a small, narrow figure that disappeared into the hulking shadows.

TWENTY

"ARE YOU SURE you don't want to stay with us?" Naomi asked as she and Luke walked the last half mile into Cascade Locks. "Bev's got plenty of room."

There was nothing Luke would have liked better than to spend more time with Naomi. The five-day section from Mt. Jefferson to Cascade Locks had been a hike of pure enjoyment. He and Naomi had been perfect hiking partners, agreeing on everything from when to start each day to how long to rest and how fast to walk. They'd been happy to hike in silence for miles, and at other times, talked nonstop.

Without saying so, they'd also agreed to sleep in their own tents. Exhausting 30-mile days hadn't stopped Luke from feeling a flicker of need every time he unrolled his sleeping bag, but each evening they unpacked two tents. That made things easier in the long run.

"Thanks, but I'll stay at the motel near the bridge. I don't want to overwhelm your friend with my laundry," replied Luke. In reality, he needed to be alone for a day to organize his thoughts and make phone calls. He hadn't for a minute forgotten about the sobering messages and intel he'd received

129

over the past few weeks. He hadn't heard from Charlie since Ashland. *No news is good news. Maybe things got resolved.*

"Okay," said Naomi as they walked toward the post office. Naomi's friend, Bev, was already at the parking lot, waiting in her car. They waved to each other. Luke noticed that Bev gave him the once-over when she got out of the car. After introductions, he touched Naomi's arm. "See you tomorrow at 8 at the bridge. Sleep well." He turned and headed for the post office.

"I'll be there, Luke," replied Naomi.

On his way out of the parking lot, Luke heard Bev remark to Naomi, "Who's the mountain man?"

He couldn't help but smile. He must not look that bad. The post office was crowded with hikers queued up for their re-supply boxes. A small group of them bent over a large bin in a corner, scavenging through food items that previous hikers had discarded to reduce pack weight. Boxes of dried soup mix and instant rice, packages of couscous and dried banana chips. Even used boots were there for the taking. His re-supply box from Marina was there, and a small, sealed envelope with his name typed on it. Luke tucked the envelope into a pocket, waved again at Naomi and Bev on his way down the street, and made his way to the Bridge of the Gods Motel.

Several other hikers were checking in. It was peak time for thru-hikers to cross into Washington, and Luke was lucky to get a room. His had a view of the bridge that crossed the Columbia River. The metal cantilevered bridge was a significant landmark for thru-hikers, signaling the last section of the PCT through the Cascade Mountains of Washington.

Luke's thoughts weren't on the view. He dumped his pack and re-supply box on the bed and opened the envelope. A short note said: *Meet me at the Pacific Crest Pub at 6 P.M. I'll have a Green Bay Packer's cap on.* It was signed *Friend of Leon's.*

A message delivered by hand. It must be serious, enough to keep Charlie from sending a message by phone or email. Alerting Leon was out of line in the first place, Luke knew, and Charlie probably didn't want to go any further. He must be pulling back and turning the reins over to Leon.

Luke had a couple of hours before he left to meet his contact. That was enough time to do a wash, have a shower, and sort through the re-supply box. Enough time, too, to call Marina, though he wasn't sure he wanted to. He didn't want to get into another fight. He hesitated, then plugged in his cell phone and punched in his home number. Grace answered.

"Hey, Gracie," said Luke, relieved. "How's my tennis star? I forgot to ask you about it last time we spoke."

"Oh, hi, Dad. Yeah, Carrie and I got to the doubles finals, but a couple of stupid bitches from Santa Barbara beat us."

Luke winced, but let it pass.

"What about work, how's that going?"

"It's okay. You'll never guess who came to the theater to watch a movie last weekend? The Smith family. You know, as in Will Smith? They were pretty nice. Didn't flaunt their celeb status too much."

"Good, Gracie. I'm glad you're sticking it out at the movie theater. Is Mom around?"

"No, she's out running. Again. Carrie's with her. She's been running a lot. She's training for a 10-K in Simi Valley or somewhere. You want me to tell her something?"

"No, just hi. I'm in Cascade Locks, at the north part of Oregon for the night. I start Washington tomorrow, Grace."

"Wow, that's great, Dad. I'll let her know."

"Tell her thanks for the box." He paused. "I couldn't have done this without all of you."

"Yeah, we know."

"Okay. Love you, Grace."

"Love you, too, Dad. Stay cool."

⁂

THE PACIFIC CREST PUB was jammed with people, mostly scruffy hikers passing through town. It was warm inside and smelled not unpleasantly of effort. A man wearing a Packer's cap sat at a small table in the corner of the pub drinking a beer. His back was to the wall. He appeared comfortable but aware, his eyes always scanning. Cops weren't hard to spot. Luke sat down and extended his hand. "Luke Chamberlin," he said.

The man smiled. "Kirby Thompson."

Luke motioned toward the hat. "You a fan?"

"No," answered Kirby. "I'm for the Seahawks, but Leon said you'd like the hat."

He handed Luke a menu. "You must be starving. I hear the chowder is great."

When the waitress returned, Luke ordered a beer, salmon chowder, a double hamburger, and fries. Kirby ordered the same, and another beer.

"Leon's been busy," he said. "He called up a bunch of JTTF members right up through Washington, looking for information, and also, for people who like to hike. You guys are certifiably nuts, by the way."

Their beers came, and Luke took a long drink from his, waiting for Kirby to continue.

"Here's what we know so far. All of the JTTFs in the western U.S. have received intel from Vancouver, by way of the Terrorist Tracking Center in D.C., stating there may be something going on along remote parts of the border between

Canada and the U.S. They don't know where or even what. There's lots of edge up there. But the likelihood of a situation is rising fast."

Luke didn't respond.

"The Feds are doing their usual song and dance routine, so the second part of Leon's message says you'll be meeting some guys at Rainy Pass, local sheriffs with JTTF experience. You'll hear more about the exact day in Stehekin—wherever that is."

Luke still said nothing.

"For some crazy reason, these guys like to hike and want to finish the last 100 miles with you. They'll just keep their eyes open. Maybe they'll hear something. Maybe not. Maybe at the border some other messages will come their way, and they'll be in a position to react. They plan to hang out a while around Manning Park in British Columbia. Do a few other hikes. Leon wants you to lead them up there."

When the chowder arrived, they both ate silently for a few minutes. "How's that sound to you?" Kirby finally asked.

"Sounds like it might complicate my hike," responded Luke. "I was counting on Charlie and Leon taking care of this. I didn't think I needed to be involved anymore."

Kirby shrugged his shoulders. "Guess they want an experienced hiker to lead the way. These men know their way around the woods, but haven't done much of the Crest Trail."

They finished eating and paid their bills. Outside the door, they shook hands.

"You got a message to relay back?" asked Kirby.

"Just that these guys better not slow me down."

Kirby smiled. "Good luck."

"Thanks," said Luke. He took his time walking back to the motel, pausing at shops and art galleries that lined Main Street. In one window he spotted a small wood carving of a raven and next to it a book about raven mythology. Ravens weren't common where they lived in Southern California, but he knew Marina liked this larger cousin of the crow. He wished the shop were still open. He'd buy both items and send them to her. But he'd be on the bridge to Washington early the next day, way before the shop opened, and he couldn't wait.

He stopped again at a park that bordered the river. In the background, lights on the Bridge of the Gods blinked the way to Washington. A museum, playground, marina, and campground welcomed visitors. He looked across the water, pondering the message he'd received at the pub. He was grateful that Charlie and Leon had come through. They had followed up correctly and found a situation. A potentially dangerous one. They'd had faith in him even if he had sounded crazy. But he hoped he'd be out of it, free to simply hike. Then there was Naomi. Could he continue to hike with her? Did he want to?

. . .

NAOMI WAS WAITING FOR HIM at the Bridge of the Gods at 8 A.M., but with jeans and a T-shirt on, and without her backpack. Bev's car was parked nearby.

"What's going on?" he asked.

Naomi gave Luke a light hug. "I've got to get off the trail for a while. A patient is failing much faster than I thought. She and her family have been asking for me. I can't let them down."

Luke hadn't meant his face to show such disappointment. "I see."

"Hey," said Naomi, "I intend to get back on the trail as soon as I can. It depends on her condition."

Luke didn't know what to say. Everything stuck in his throat. He scribbled his cell phone number on a scrap of paper and handed it to her.

"Let me know if you do," he said.

"To be sure, Luke," said Naomi. She turned for Bev's car. "Don't get lost."

Luke returned a lopsided smile. Then he stepped up onto the bridge.

TWENTY-ONE

MAHMOUD STOOD unsteadily on the dock, shivering in the cool, damp night. The sweatshirt he wore over his T-shirt and the red skull cap Masood had given him in Karachi provided little warmth.

The change in weather had been a minor shock compared to the Pacific crossing. Although time on fishing boats had helped him grow sea legs, he'd been overwhelmed by the vastness of the ocean and the size of the waves that picked up the huge container ship and tossed her back down in gut-twisting rolls. He was proud, though, that he'd spent only two days in his bunk. The rest of the time, he'd been able to do his job as one of a dozen or so deck hands, chipping paint and handling lines. It had been boring, but he'd blended in, with the help of an officer friendly to the cause. Any time there was a question about what to do or where to go, the officer would appear with an answer.

At Vancouver's port, Mahmoud had been coiling a line when a Canadian customs and immigration agent walked up the gangplank. He hadn't known what the uniform on the man meant, only that he was an official person. He'd felt a

137

prick of fear and pulled the hood of his sweatshirt over his head. He shrank against the side of a container, watching the agent enter the bridge and speak to the captain. The man had taken the crew list, looked it over, scribbled something down and handed it back. Mahmoud was flooded with relief as the agent left the ship.

Now, he stood among the forest of containers standing on the pier, as directed by the officer who had helped him on the ship. He glanced over his shoulder and shivered again. The ship loomed behind him, quiet now, and still. He wondered about the next part of his journey—if there was a next part. And if so, would he board a ship again. He would go to the ends of the earth for Allah, but he hoped it wouldn't involve another ship.

Mahmoud watched two headlights bounce down the pier toward him. A beat-up Toyota stopped, and a red-haired man with a full beard got out of the car. "Greetings, Mahmoud," he said in Arabic. "I am Salem. Do you have the box?"

Mahmoud took a step back. He had seen Egyptians like the blue-eyed, red-headed Salem before. They were offspring of European crusaders who had occupied their Holy Land a thousand years ago. Mahmoud thought they were crazy and didn't trust them. He clutched the backpack closer. "It's here, in the backpack," he responded, also in Arabic.

"Good," replied Salem. He peered closely at Mahmoud. "You look like shit. Get into the car. We'll get you a cup of tea. A proper jacket, too."

Salem said nothing more as they drove through the gloom of Vancouver's harbor and into the city. Even though it was dark, Mahmoud felt the same awe that he'd had driving through Karachi. He gawked at the tall buildings and busy streets. Here, there were differences. The cars were larger. Not just a few, but all of the women wore western-style clothing.

And the city was draped in lushness with trees, grass, or flowers growing on every street. Most surprising to Mahmoud, the air was clean.

In a few minutes, the view deteriorated as they entered a poorer part of the city. Salem stopped the car in front of a decaying apartment building on East Hastings Street, a rundown section of Vancouver. A man wrapped in a blanket huddled on a doorstep. A woman in a short skirt, heels, and a tight leather tank top stood at a corner, smoking, staring at nothing. Mahmoud lowered his eyes as he got out of the car.

He followed Salem up two flights of stairs into a shabby, smoky apartment. Against one wall, a couch had been draped with a blanket in an attempt to cover up holes and tears in the upholstery. Cotton innards still spilled out from the corners. The floors were bare, and the two windows dirty with dust and city scum. Several prayer rugs were rolled up in a corner. A door led to what Mahmoud surmised was the bedroom. The opposite wall served as the kitchen with a counter, sink, refrigerator, and stove. The sink, full of unwashed dishes, stank. Mahmoud thought even the shack his family lived in was better than this.

A small table to one side was covered with folders, maps, a computer, and cell phones. Compared to the rest of the room, it was neat and clean.

Two other men were waiting in the apartment. One was a westerner, tall, blond, and clean-shaven. He wore blue jeans and a sweatshirt with a Canucks hockey team emblem on it. He nodded to Mahmoud. The other man was smaller, dark, and with a beard. "Hello, Mahmoud," he said in Urdu. "I am Raheem. How was your trip?"

Mahmoud recognized him as a Pakistani and breathed easier.

"I'm here," he replied in Urdu.

Raheem smiled. "You are so young. I have a son your age, back in Karachi."

He took Mahmoud by the shoulders. "You are very brave. You have the courage of 1,000 lions," he said.

Mahmoud's heart lifted. In Islam, the lion was a symbol of strength, courage, and force. He no longer felt the damp cold. He held his head high.

"Can I see the backpack?" asked Raheem.

Mahmoud gave it to the Pakistani. It was strange, to no longer hold something he hadn't let out of his hands for weeks, something he had guarded with his life. Yet, he felt the physical weight replaced with pride.

"Enough of the ocean, hey?" said Salem, offering Mahmoud tea. He added with a wide grin, "Are you ready for a walk in the mountains?"

*   *   *

SO THERE WOULD BE MORE TO HIS MISSION. Even with this Egyptian as company, he would continue with honor. "That, I can do," he replied.

TWENTY-TWO

L UKE THREW HIMSELF into the log shelter off the trail a few miles beyond Stampede Pass. It was new and roughly put together, but tight enough to keep him dry. It had rained on and off the past two weeks, and he thought he'd go crazy if he didn't get out of it. The guide was right about the southern Cascades—when you can see Mt. Rainier, it's going to rain. When you can't see the mountain, it is raining. A poncho that covered both him and his pack was by far the best piece of gear he had brought.

On this section, the PCT had produced spectacular views—when the clouds dislodged from the sky enough so he could see. The trail had passed the snowy sentries of Mt. Adams and Mt. St. Helens and then plunged into Goat Rocks Wilderness. Luke had tried to ignore the weather. He'd tackled the trail in the rugged wilderness and despite the fog and drizzle, had glimpsed a group of elusive mountain goats for which the area was named. With cushioned, skid-proof pads on their feet, they galloped over cliffs and leaped across crevices—moves that made even the most seasoned climber envious. And then mighty Mt. Rainier came into view, appearing and disappearing as Luke trekked toward Snoqualmie Pass. The mountain seemed omnipresent, like a god. He wondered if it watched over him, or simply watched him.

When Luke started this section, he'd been more unsettled at Naomi's absence than he'd expected. That gait, those long legs, her laugh—he missed her. But in a few days, he'd found his own rhythm again and felt relieved at not having to battle his conscience. As miles passed, the image of her face had faded a little. He'd concluded that his feelings were a by-product of the trail and its isolation from family and his former life—or at least that was what he told himself.

Luke rolled his mat and sleeping bag onto the floor of the shelter. He was a little surprised that no other hikers were there. Dozens of miserable people, like him, were out there, searching for a dry spot. Then he took off his boots and dug around in his pack to find something that resembled dry clothes. He found his long underwear, stripped off his damp shirt and shorts and pulled them on.

Next, a hot meal. He heated water on the gas stove and broke out a package of freeze-dried beef stew. After the stew and a cup of tea, he started to warm up.

In his rush to get dry, he hadn't noticed a notebook in a plastic bag hung on a wall of the shelter—hiker messages. Luke took the notebook off the wall to browse while he still had light. The messages were written in chronological order, starting from several months ago. Some were hikers' thoughts and impressions. Some were drawings or poems. Others warned of wash-outs or areas with little water. Luke scanned them and stopped at one titled: To Camper, From Sea Dog: *Here on September 1. Rain. Off last time at Snoqualmie Pass. Should bump into you at Stehekin.*

Luke smiled. It'd be good to hike with Mike again, especially with other men tagging along. Even though he hardly knew

Mike, he trusted the SEAL. It was more than being able to count on him, like he had at the Belden Gorge Saloon. Maybe it was the military connection, their training, their loyalty to a cause. Maybe it was just a good gut feeling about the guy.

Luke finished his tea. He'd call Mike at Snoqualmie Pass tomorrow. It was time to tell him what was going on, and he hoped Mike would have the time and be open to joining what now looked like a reconnoitering team.

He'd also make another phone call. After Cascade Locks, he'd reviewed in his head who knew what. Charlie obviously hadn't gotten the FBI interested yet, but had contacted the JTTF. They thought there was enough positive intel to send some guys along on his hike. But then Charlie must have had to lay low. Luke wouldn't contact him again. Another old associate, Ken Savage at the U.S. Justice Inspector General's Office, was trustworthy, and he cared. Ken might be able to light a fire under the Feds. They had to get on board.

Luke closed the notebook and replaced it in its plastic bag on the wall. He cleaned up and put his dishes outside the shelter to wash in the rain. His feet had started to swell again, and he swallowed a couple of ibuprofen. *Maybe nothing is ahead*, he thought, rubbing them. *Only the end of the trail. Then what.* He didn't know, but he remembered Mike's words around a campfire in the Sierras, that there was more to a good relationship than coming home a hero. He wondered if he knew how to be anything else.

Luke got into his sleeping bag. It grew dark earlier now that it was September, and he wanted to write in his journal. Just as he finished detailing the day's efforts, he heard a sharp whistle. He leaned out of the shelter and watched a marmot waddle into the campsite. Without any hesitation the large rodent made for his trekking poles leaning against the shelter and started to nibble on the salty, leather straps. "Hey, get lost," Luke shouted. The hungry marmot continued to chew vigorously. Luke picked up a small rock from a corner of the shelter and threw it, meaning to scare the marmot off. "I said, get lost!"

The rock hit the marmot's paw. It yelped and sat back on its hind legs, raising its paw as if to say, "Why did you do that?" Then it limped away.

Luke dragged his poles into the shelter. "Serves you right," he grumbled. He returned to his sleeping bag and listened to the rain dance on the shelter's roof. He suddenly felt sorry he'd hurt the animal. Marina was always going on about animal totems. Although she wasn't Native American, in the brief time she'd known his grandfather, she'd absorbed his stories and read about the strong symbology of animals. A squirrel meant this and a crow meant that. A marmot probably was the god of something or other, its appearance a sign. Luke closed his eyes. *The trail's getting to you.*

Luke woke to a cloudy sky but one without rain. He gulped down a bowl of granola, mixed only with powdered milk, powdered honey, cocoa, and water, then repacked his damp gear. Fifteen miles to Snoqualmie Pass and a motel with a laundry and restaurant. He couldn't get there fast enough.

The terrain the trail followed changed from subalpine parklands sparkling with lakes, to land shredded by logging, though it wasn't nearly as desecrated as other hikers had warned. Wildflowers bloomed in the meadows and alongside the streams, and the clear-cut areas were covered with bright red huckleberry and dark blueberry bushes. They grew so thickly along this part of the trail that logging roads were lined with cars and nearby fields full of people picking them. Luke half expected to see bears eating right alongside. He took a few minutes to stop and fill his cereal bowl.

By early afternoon, he passed under the lift of the Snoqualmie Pass Ski Area. He left the trail and walked directly down the slope to a large white building with a red roof—the Best Western. A number of hikers were checking in and out, and Luke got in line, grateful to stand where it was warm.

His room was on the second floor and overlooked the parking lot. He dumped his damp belongings from the pack and sorted clothes from gear. He started a load in the laundry, shaved, and took a long, hot shower. He decided against cutting his hair, and left it tied back at the nape of his neck.

After a meal at the restaurant, he felt human again. It was 8 P.M. On his way back to the room, he stopped at the hotel shop and bought a bottle of wine. In his room, he poured a glass, and called Marina. It was a quick conversation, mostly about the girls.

Then he punched in Sea Dog's number.

"Sea Dog. It's Luke. Got your message at Stampede Pass. Where are you?"

"Camper. Wondered when I'd hear from you. I'm at a campsite a couple of days from Stehekin. How 'bout you?"

"I'm at Snoqualmie. Glad to be out of the rain. It's been bad."

"Yeah, tell me about it."

"Look, are you in a hurry to finish? Your sponsors putting any pressure on you?"

"Nah, I'm ahead of schedule. Why?"

"I'm involved in a little trail project, and I'd like your company."

"A trail project?" Mike waited for more details, but none came. "You don't mean trail maintenance, do you."

"No. A small reconnoiter. I'll tell you more about it if you can hang around Stehekin until I get there."

"Recon's my specialty, Luke."

"I thought so."

"I can hardly wait to hear about it. See you in a few days."

Luke poured a second glass of wine and jotted down the salient information Ken needed to make further inquiries into the terrorist threat. He found the channel changer and clicked on the news and weather. More rain.

The next morning, he called Ken and got off the phone before the federal investigator could object to his plan. He ate breakfast, then retrieved his re-supply box at the post office, and packed up.

By mid-morning, he stood in the lobby's check-out line. A tall, slender woman walked over. "Hi, Luke," said Naomi. "I figured you'd be here about now."

TWENTY-THREE

KEN SAVAGE hung up the phone and swung his chair around to face the window. Outside his Pasadena office, a few people sat listlessly under shady trees in the 100-plus-degree day. To the east, the San Bernardino Mountains and Angeles National Forest reached into the cool air above the yellow layer of smog that blanketed Pasadena and most of the Los Angeles Basin. Still, the mostly perfect weather made him glad he'd transferred from New York's gray, cold climate to Southern California. The culture was another matter, however. Ken worked hard to keep himself trim, a must in this part of the state where growing old was frowned upon. He colored his graying hair and worried about his teen-aged daughter who was asking for a large tattoo of a phoenix in the middle of her back for her 14th birthday. At least, he thought with some relief, she wasn't requesting Botox treatment, like some of her friends.

Ken worked with the Inspector General's Office for the western region. He investigated any violation of rules within in the Department of Justice's agencies, including the FBI.

147

Currently, he was involved in a case over at the federal prison. A guard was caught beating up a prisoner after the prisoner threw a bag of feces at him. He nearly put out the prisoner's eye, but the other guards weren't talking. A typical scenario. He was working jointly with the FBI, which was investigating the case as a civil rights violation. It was going to be a long, sticky investigation. Ken enjoyed good working relationships with other agencies, and these cases always made him feel uncomfortable.

And now there was this bizarre phone call from Luke Chamberlin. He knew Luke well. He'd worked for him in Newark's FBI office before deciding to leave the Bureau for the Inspector General's Office.

Ken tapped his pencil on the desk. What a story. An unknown terrorist threat coming into the country, possibly from Vancouver, perhaps headed, as Luke deduced, to San Francisco or Los Angeles. And he'd gotten this from an old Soviet nemesis? And then told Charlie Logan at the FBI? And plans to snoop around the northern part of the PCT with some rogue law enforcers? What the hell had gotten into him? Luke, the agent who'd retired early and not exactly happy. Luke, who's supposed to be enjoying the trip of his life. Ken shook his head. Good old Luke—too conscientious, too caring, unable to let go of the past.

Ken tapped his pencil harder. If things turned ugly, what would Luke do then? Ken remembered Luke admitting over a beer in a Newark bar that he didn't like to shoot his gun, even though he had always qualified with a decent score. Something about his grandfather being the victim of a shooting. Luke had attended the FBI Academy several years earlier than Ken, and by the time Ken arrived, Luke had garnered quite a reputation with his tomahawk. Seems he was convinced to take groups of interested agent candidates to the woods beyond the abandoned Hoover Road where he entertained them with remarkable throws at trees, at logs, at the smallest stump.

What good would a tomahawk be in a shoot-out with people who didn't mind in the slightest if they died? Then he remembered a guy who could help in that department. Lewis Hamada, a Forest Service law enforcement ranger he knew. Special agents like Lewis patrolled forest lands in uniforms and carried firearms. Just like other law enforcement officers, they executed search warrants, made arrests, and testified in court. Lewis also happened to be an expert shot. He knew rangers and the areas they patrolled up the West Coast into Washington and could give Luke information about any suspicious activities on Forest Service land. And offer fire power, if he needed it.

Ken considered more of their conversation. Luke said he'd spoken to Charlie. Who else had he contacted? And more to the point, why wasn't the FBI on the case? And if they were, why hadn't he heard about it? After 9/11, the FBI should be investigating any intel, no matter how slight the information—particularly if it pointed to militant cells. He thought back to the World Trade Center towers in 1993 and the millennium bomber in 2000. If terrorists were behind it, they wouldn't give up until the mission was completed.

Ken sighed. Director Mulberry relished making the news with parental kidnappings and kiddy porn investigations and arrests—subjects with huge public interest. Rumor had it that Mulberry's eyes glazed over when briefed about a major intelligence case or the start of the bank failures a few years ago. The Bureau had shifted much of its resources over to terrorism and made those investigations a number one priority. Yet, terrorism not only was too big for the Bureau and other intelligence agencies to get their arms around, the investigations also were often secret and unavailable to the public. Information sharing continued to be a problem amongst the dozens of agencies collecting intelligence.

Ken looked at his watch. First, he'd call Lewis. Get him connected with the local JTTFs Leon had rounded up. Then he'd call Carol Linderman at the U.S. Attorney's Office. Her office was in charge of L.A.'s JTTF and maybe she'd heard something. If not, she had the authority to find out from the FBI.

❖   ❖   ❖

CAROL LINDERMAN HUNG UP THE PHONE, her face lined with a grimace. Her conversation with Ken had been brief.

A possible threat originating in Vancouver. A rogue group of law enforcement officers doing their own investigation. How could I not know about this?

She looked up Bill Scully's number. "Bill? Carol Linderman at the U.S. Attorney's Office."

"Yes, I'm fine." Carol cut the small talk. "Looks like we've got a situation here. You heard anything about a possible terrorist threat to the U.S.? You have? Something vague? Where's Jen? Well, call her on the golf course and have her contact me immediately. I want all the details, and, specifically, I want to know why I haven't been kept informed of this."

Carol slammed the phone onto its cradle. "Great," she muttered under her breath. "Another fuck-up at the FBI. It's never been the same over there since Luke left."

TWENTY-FOUR

MARY LOU opened the door to the guardhouse. "Go on out," she said to Pinot, who sniffed the morning air and walked carefully into the rocky yard.

Mary Lou found her binoculars and followed the cat outside. Although satellites pinpointed fires now, it had been a dry winter, and with the scars of the three-year-old fire still blackening the pass, she was extra vigilant. Nothing like a good pair of binoculars to see what needed to be seen.

She lifted her powerful Nikons and scanned the hills. As she viewed the area to her left, she noticed that a primitive campsite, about a quarter mile away, wasn't empty—the first time in over three years. The burned-out area had simply been too unappealing for campers. She adjusted the binoculars for a closer look.

Three tents were pitched around a dead fire pit with a familiar-looking pick-up truck parked nearby. The tents were an old canvas military style, not the kind backpackers or even campers used these days. Mary Lou noticed that there were no boots, trekking poles, or backpacks lying around. Peculiar. People just didn't come to Harts Pass to hang out in vintage tents. And it was still a bit early to see hawks.

Two men were bringing things from the truck to the tents and came into Mary Lou's view. While they wore casual clothes, they certainly weren't hikers.

I know them. They were here a few weeks ago asking about the hawks. Why are they back so soon? And not where I told them to go, over near Slate Peak?

Mary Lou had about an hour before she made her daily phone call to the Forest Service in Mazama. She decided to find out a little more about who was camping in her part of the Cascades. She put on her hat, jumped into her jeep and headed down the rutted dirt road toward the campsite.

*   *   *

"HELLO," SHE SAID, PULLING UP TO THE SITE a few minutes later. "I see you decided to come back, even without the hawks."

The clean-shaven westerner, the one who had spoken at the guardhouse, walked toward her. "Yes," he said, "we decided to come anyway—for some peace and quiet. A rest you might say."

"I see," replied Mary Lou. "Well, camping here costs $10.00 a night. How many nights are you staying?"

"We're not sure. A few, maybe more," he said, taking out his wallet. He handed Mary Lou several bills. "Will this cover a week?"

"A week?" said Mary Lou, taking the money. "Why on earth would you want to stay here a week?"

The men stiffened. The one speaking to Mary Lou narrowed his eyes. "A rest, we need a quiet place to rest. Is there a problem?"

Mary Lou heard the tightness and slight threat in his voice. "No, not at all," she replied. She counted the bills. "I'll leave you to your resting." She gave them a pamphlet about dos and don'ts for camping in a National Forest and turned back to the jeep.

"Thanks," said the westerner, waving the pamphlet after her. "We'll be sure to follow the rules."

His response sent a shiver up Mary Lou's spine. She climbed into the jeep without replying and left the campsite.

On the way back to the guardhouse, she thought about the campsite. Two men, only one of whom spoke, at a smelly, burned-out site. Outdated equipment and not enough of it for camping more than a couple of nights. For more than that, people usually brought large tents, chairs, a gas stove—their kitchen sink if they could. Their reappearance struck Mary Lou as strange enough to mention in her morning call to the Forest Service in Mazama.

TWENTY-FIVE

LUKE HAD HIKED 2,500 miles. Another hundred and he'd be in Canada. He glanced back at Naomi, who walked slightly behind him. Her lips were parted and sweat streaked her face. She smiled at him, and the sun, finally showing itself again, ignited her red-blond hair. What would he do with her? He'd been shocked to see her at the Best Western. He didn't think she'd get back to the trail once she got off. But there she was, in the lobby, with her backpack on. While he had stared at her new shaggy haircut, she had reported on her two weeks off the trail tending to a dying patient. She had offered a lot of detail. "The room wasn't dark, Luke. No drapes pulled at this house. No drapes at all. Her cat, Fluffy, stayed on her bed nearly the whole day. She refused to get off. Toward the end, a woman came into the room and sang..."

She had gone on and on, and he had only half listened. Instead, he'd ticked off in his mind the things he needed to do at Stehekin: get supplies; meet Mike; make a plan; pray that a message waited, explaining that the threat had been a hoax.

He had stuck to his conclusion at Cascade Locks that Naomi's charm was due to his separation from Marina. But after

155

a day with Naomi, that convincing conclusion had dissolved as quickly as salt in water. This past week, they had slipped back to their amiable hiking pattern, walking and talking, leaving no subject unturned. God, it had felt good. He'd recalled another of Granddad's stories about the Chippewa. They believed that a person's spirit connected to other spirits on a level that didn't exist anywhere else. An instant understanding resulted. Luke was beginning to wonder if this was happening to him.

Whatever his feelings were, they'd grown stronger each day he'd walked beside Naomi. Even so, they'd managed to keep their hands off each other. Naomi had clearly stated she respected Luke's marriage. She hadn't received the same respect from her own husband. She never made an overture. They said good night from their own tents, and after a joke or funny comment, they both went to sleep.

Luke and Naomi heard the sound of rushing water even though they weren't yet close to the Suiattle River. The bridge crossing the fast-running Suiattle had washed out several years ago. With heavy rains plaguing the area the past few days, they knew fording it would be tough.

"Uh-oh," said Naomi, when they reached the river, "This doesn't look good. That water must be up to my waist."

Glacier sediments washing down from mountainsides had turned the water milky white. It swirled around barely exposed rocks and churned up tiny whirlpools. It made the creeks he'd tottered over in the Sierras seem pint-sized.

Luke walked closer to the bank. He recalled an article he'd read in a hiking magazine a few months ago. An experienced hiker had tried to ford a fast-running river near Mt. Hood, very much like this one, and ended up a wet corpse. She hadn't loosened the waist belt on her backpack before crossing—something any good hiker knows to do—and then had lost her footing. The tightly cinched pack had held her face down in the water. She was found washed up on the river bank a mile down the river, her backpack still on.

Luke looked downstream and made out boot prints leading to a narrow log. "Let's check this out," he said to Naomi.

The log, about 20 feet long, wasn't much thicker than a person, and even though boot traffic showed it had been crossed a number of times, the bark was covered with moss and appeared wet and slippery. Underneath, the water surged through a narrowing of the riverbed. With the nearest road and help 30 miles away, this was not a place to lose footing.

His experience with earlier fords and better judgment told Luke to look for another way to cross, maybe at a shallower section. Granddad said never be in a hurry in the woods. But he was in a hurry. Then he had an idea.

"I think we can do this," he said to Naomi. "We can scoot across on our butts."

Naomi put her hands on her hips and peered closely at the log. "I don't know, Luke. It looks treacherous."

"Not if we do it right," replied Luke. "I think I did this once in the Boy Scouts," he added with a wink. "I'll go first."

Luke unbuckled the waist belt of his pack and straddled the log, one leg dangling on either side. Placing his two hands on the log in front of him, he lifted himself up and forward. Up and forward. Up and forward.

On the other side, he called to Naomi, "It's a little rough on the hands, but you'll do fine. Come on."

Naomi undid her pack's waist belt and straddled the log. She began scooting across as she'd seen Luke do. Halfway over, her right pant leg caught on a small broken branch off the side of the log. She tried to shake her pant loose, but the branch held fast. She was stuck.

Naomi took her right hand off the front of the log to pull the material off the stump.

"Keep both hands on!" called Luke.

Naomi looked up at Luke, but the sound of the water smothered his words.

As Naomi twisted a little farther to get a better grip on the material, her pack shifted slightly to the right. Already off balance, this shift was enough to pull her off the log. She toppled into the water and tumbled downstream. She grabbed at rocks and stumps of trees but couldn't hold on. Every time she tried to stand, the water pushed her over.

Luke tore off his backpack and scrambled along the banks. "Take your pack off, Naomi!" he yelled. "Let it go!"

Naomi heard him. She tried to find good footing to shrug off the pack, but again and again she was knocked over and tossed around like a rag doll. Finally, she half swam, half dragged herself to the side of the river.

Luke got ahead of her and stuck his trekking pole out into the water. "Grab this," he said as Naomi struggled close. But she missed as an eddy pulled her under. *Jesus, her pack is going to hold her under.*

Then he saw her head come up and she reached for a rock, clutching it with both hands. "Luke," she shouted, "I can't hold on."

Luke grabbed one of his trekking poles and waded into the water. Foot entrapment was a common cause of death on rivers. A foot caught between rocks caused panic, then a fast current did the rest. He took a deep breath. Using the pole to steady himself, he navigated carefully through the water. *It has to be three feet deep*, he thought grimly. He saw that for the moment, Naomi's pack had jammed her against a couple of rocks, but the force of the water was loosening it. He faced upstream and pushed his legs hard against the current, shuffling his boots along the bottom. He was moving too slowly. Naomi was slipping off the rock.

The image of a bear suddenly appeared to Luke. Granddad had read many stories to him about bears, an animal of strength and courage. Luke thought back to the Sierras. He had survived an encounter with a bear, and according to the Chippewa, had thus gained its strength. Luke took a deep breath and steadied himself, forcing his legs to move faster. He would not let Naomi face the same fate of the hiker lost last year.

"Got you!" Luke shouted as he reached Naomi.

"About time, Mountain Man," Naomi's voice was barely audible.

Luke unbuckled Naomi's chest strap. The pack could go. He grabbed her around the waist and pulled her up. "Hold on to me," he said.

Moving at a slower pace, they carefully retraced his steps until they reached the bank.

"I'm okay, I'm okay," Naomi gasped, collapsing on the river bank.

"Well," said Luke, "at least you're on the right side of the river."

Naomi glared at his effort at humor, but she managed a smile.

Naomi's pack had gotten tangled up again, this time in branches not far from the bank. Luke left Naomi with directions to take off her wet clothes and put on some of his, and fetched her pack.

When he returned, Naomi hadn't changed and was shivering uncontrollably. Tears rolled down her cheeks. Luke held her while she cried.

His comforting murmurs turned into a kiss on her cold face. She didn't resist.

"Hey," said Luke softly, "let's get your stuff out and dry. We don't have to make Stehekin today. We'll camp here."

Luke set up his tent and started a fire. He heated water for tea and a hot meal. He peered into the tent. Naomi was taking off her wet clothes.

"Your clothes are wet, too, Luke."

He started to strip them off, aware of Naomi's eyes lingering on his chest. Under her gaze, his heart pounded.

Something lying on the floor of the tent caught his attention. The crow feather. He stared at it. Where had it come from?

"Luke?" Naomi touched his shoulder and ran her finger down his chest.

Luke abruptly stopped undressing. He found dry clothes in his pack and gave them to Naomi. He put on a dry shirt and grabbed the wet clothes. "I'll get these drying by the fire," he said and ducked out of the tent.

Naomi came out in a few minutes. She sat by the fire in Luke's clothes. She'd stopped shivering. He handed her a bowl of hot stew.

He had spread the wet contents of her pack on the ground, including a small notebook. He noticed her staring at it. "Didn't read a single page," he said, struggling to be light.

Naomi didn't reply. She ate the stew in silence, but when she saw he had laid out the tent's rain cover on the other side of the fire, she gave him a questioning look.

"I'll sleep out here," he said, downing his tea.

He stood up and threw more wood on the fire.

TWENTY-SIX

L UKE AND NAOMI sat at a picnic table next to the bakery outside Stehekin. Famous for its cinnamon rolls, the bakery was highlighted in all the PCT guides as a not-to-be-missed spot. But Naomi and Luke only picked at their rolls, avoiding each other's eyes.

That morning, Luke had woken stiff and cold next to the dead fire. Naomi was already up, making cereal and tea, herself again. They hadn't spoken much the rest of the way to Stehekin. They didn't discuss the near disaster at the river. Luke had told her he was meeting friends and staying in town a couple of days. That he had planned to finish the trail with them. It was weak, he knew, but Naomi had accepted the explanation. She had implicitly understood what he was really trying to say and had not objected.

She had her own deadline. She needed to return to her job by the third week in September, so she couldn't take any zero days. At the bakery she had changed into a pair of trail runners, which, while not as sturdy, were lighter than boots and together with a light pack, might allow her another mile or two per day. One of her shoes was held together with duct tape. "Can't afford new ones," she'd explained, when he'd asked her about it.

"Well," said Naomi, finishing her roll, "let's head to town." Her eyes suddenly fixed on his. She grabbed his hand. "Luke, let's take the ferry out of Stehekin. We'll go somewhere else for a while and be together. We can finish the trail later."

Luke was stunned. He hadn't expected this, especially after the previous evening, but the intensity of her words bore into him. He held her gaze, then squeezed her hand. "Part of me can't think of anything I'd rather do. But I can't."

Naomi lowered her head. Then she looked back up at Luke, her features carefully composed, as if she'd put on a mask. "Yeah, I know." She opened her mouth to say something else, but stopped. Instead, she withdrew her hand from Luke's.

"I'll be putting in long days, maybe a couple of 30-milers, so I don't know if you'll catch me. Particularly with that thing," she added, motioning to his pack.

"We'll see about that," Luke replied. In his mind, though, he knew he wouldn't catch up to her. He wouldn't even try.

Luke and Naomi walked the mile from the bakery into town. Stehekin perched on the north end of Lake Chelan, a long tail-of-a-lake tucked into the Cascades, accessible only by foot, horse, ferry, or seaplane. It was out of the way for many vacationers but thru-hikers often stayed a few extra days for the good food and a chance to rest up before the last 100 miles.

Both had re-supply packages waiting for them at the post office. Naomi grabbed hers and turned to Luke. "See you, Luke." She wrapped her arms around him. Luke hugged her, laying his cheek on top of her head. Naomi left the post office and walked up the road toward the store.

"Hey," shouted Luke, leaning out the door, "mark which way to go at the junctions, can you? You know how I tend to get confused at them."

Naomi swung her head back around. "Sure, Luke."

Besides his re-supply box, Luke had an envelope waiting. *Good, a message from Charlie.* He found a private bench outside and opened the envelope. The paper inside was covered in numbers. No words. A code, he thought, probably from Charlie. He must be worried about risking contact. He studied the numbers. What code did he and Charlie know? They'd both been schooled in cryptography but neither had spent any time with the FBI's cryptanalyst unit. Luke thought for a minute. It came to him. Charlie's son and his daughters had shared a book about spies throughout history. The first spy, Aphra Behn, lived in the 1600s and despite her sex, had been an excellent secret agent. Her story had contained the actual numbered code she'd used 400 years ago. The kids had had a lot of fun making up messages using Behn's cipher, challenging their fathers to decode them. That had to be it. Luke took out a pencil and scribbled on the back of the envelope. He scrutinized Charlie's message, dated a week ago:

"New Pakistani intel points to dirty bomb crossing into U.S. at remote Canadian border. Stay low. Help coming. Local JTTF and sharpshooting forest ranger."

A heaviness crept into Luke's stomach. *Jesus, Gennady was right. Thank God Charlie and Ken believed me. Thank God.*

Charlie's message said to stay low. Fine with him. He and his new friends might have a chance to poke around at the border, do some listening at the lodge at Manning Provincial Park, maybe see something unusual to report to the Royal Canadian Mounted Police. That would be it. He was still resolved to stay clear of any further involvement.

From around the corner came a familiar face. "Hey, Luke," grinned Mike. They shook hands. "Who's the lovely lady? I saw her give you an awfully big hug."

"It's a long story," replied Luke.

"I'll bet. Let's get some lunch," said Mike. They walked to the small café near the docks and ordered sandwiches.

"Thanks for your vote of confidence," said Luke. "I know this all sounds a little crazy."

"Yeah, well, as I said, I have the time. And frankly, I don't like the thought of a dirty bomb floating around any part of this country. Even the idea bothers me. What's the plan?"

"Like I mentioned when I called you, we're meeting some local law enforcement with connections to the JTTF from the Seattle area, and also a forest ranger, in Rainy Pass. They like to walk, and it sounds like they can keep up with us. A message I just got from a friend at the Bureau indicates that the threat—if there is one—might be near a border in Canada. Our job will be to keep our eyes and ears open and report any suspicious activity. Help is coming, supposedly."

Lunch arrived, and they dug into the sandwiches.

"Sounds pretty straightforward," said Mike.

"I don't know," said Luke. "I have a gut feeling about this, and it's not good."

He touched his stomach with his hand. "I inherited this feeling from my grandfather. It's never ever been wrong. Never."

"Huh," grunted Mike. He had worked with a SEAL like Luke once, and the guy really hadn't ever been wrong. Mike had learned to trust that gut feeling.

"What about this forest ranger, Luke?" asked Mike. "What's he going to do, be the look-out?"

"No. This guy's supposedly a real good shot. He might come in handy."

Mike shrugged his shoulders.

"The locals," Luke continued, "will hopefully know the area. And then there's you—you can do anything, right?"

Another grin. "Sure, you name it." Mike continued in a low voice, "Speaking of that, I thought we might be short on fire power, just in case we do bump into some unfriendlies. So some buddies of mine loaned me these." He patted a canvas bag at his side. ".40-caliber model 22 Glocks—they should do the trick—if we need a trick."

Luke frowned at Mike. "How did you get those here?"

"I told you, some buddies just brought them up, you know, on the ferry from Chelan."

"The ferry?" asked Luke. "The one packed with people?"

"That's right, the ferry. No sweat. You're not afraid of guns, are you?"

Luke paused. "No, I just don't want any innocent people to get hurt. We're supposed to do a little investigating and pass on any suspicious information to local law enforcement. Not play gunslingers."

"You just worry about the logistics. And keep that sixth sense honed."

"Yeah, yeah, alright." Luke opened a bag of chips. "I rented a cabin out at the dude ranch for the night. It's only a few miles from the trailhead. We can go over this again later."

"You got a cabin tonight? Great. I'm tired of sleeping on the ground. And I can't wait to hear all about the tall lady."

Mike stood up. "Hey," he said, putting money on the table. "You know what Stehekin means?"

"No," replied Luke.

"A way through, Luke. A way through."

TWENTY-SEVEN

THE PATH leading from Canada south to Monument 78, the northern terminus of the Pacific Crest Trail, ran along ridges thick with forest. Cedar and fir trees towered over Mahmoud's head. He stopped to finger the soft yellow needles of the larch trees, which splashed the landscape with gold. The vegetation, so different from the sparse shrubs that dotted the hills near his home, astounded him. His family—he hadn't been able to contact them since July. The separation had, at first, proved harder than he thought. He'd yearned to tell them about the huge fish in the Arabian Sea, his seasickness, the cities he'd seen, the inspired soldiers of Allah he'd met. But then he'd realized they simply couldn't understand. And he'd stopped feeling homesick. There was nothing back in Pakistan for him. He had completed his education and was ready to move forward, to help found a new Islamic world.

The men he followed were part of a group called the First Brigade of Islam. It was a small but active and well-funded militant cell out of Vancouver with connections that stretched to a radical Islamic movement in Kyrgyzstan. Although Mahmoud still didn't feel comfortable around the red-headed Salem, the men seemed to like him, and Mahmoud hoped he'd be able to stay with them and join the Brigade once this mission was over. He would assimilate into Vancouver. He would learn English and continue to fight.

So far, their mission had been well planned by the Brigade. They had driven to Manning Provincial Park, a hiking and Nordic ski center just north of the Canada-United States border, and left the car there, as did many people who visited the area. An eight-mile walk along a dirt road and trail brought them to the wooded, remote border. After the attack on the Twin Towers on 9/11, the Royal Canadian Mounted Police had monitored the crossing for several months, but now it stood empty.

Mahmoud carried his small pack, still unaware of its contents. At the apartment, he had asked for it back. Salem had laughed, but the Pakistani man called Raheem had returned it and spoken sharply to Salem. Once they reached Harts Pass, they were to give the pack to the second half of the team, who would be camping near the pass. These men would drive it down the road to the town of Winthrop and transport it out of Washington. Other Brigade members would then take over for the final leg of its long journey. Mahmoud would return to Canada the way he'd come.

Salem explained they didn't know the entire plan, but he believed the backpack was headed to Los Angeles International Airport to complete the mission attempted during the millennium when their Muslim brothers were stopped by a U.S. Customs agent at Port Angeles and arrested. It was safer not to know, he'd said. That way, if one were caught, he wouldn't know everything if interrogated by authorities. Nor would any one member be tempted to sell out.

The Brigade did know that the final step in the plan would bring chaos to the Americans and glory to Allah and Muslims worldwide. Mahmoud was impressed with the skills of the Brigade in devising a plan that could not possibly fail. It was simple and brilliant.

The men reached Monument 78 and stopped. No other hikers were there, though boot prints showed that some had recently passed by. The four-foot monument looked like a miniature copy of the Washington Monument in D.C. It was strung with Tibetan peace flags. One of the men kicked it. Salem unzipped his pants and urinated on it. The top of the monument was slightly ajar, and Salem lifted it off. Thru-hikers had left notes inside the tower as mementos of their trips. The men took the papers out, and while only Salem could read or speak English, they all knew the notes were of some importance. One of the other men took the notes 20 yards away where he set fire to them, laughing. As Mahmoud watched his companions stomp on the ashes, he felt a twinge. Monuments were a testament to a struggle, no matter the country or people. Why should he have regret for infidels? Ridiculous. Mahmoud shook his head and started walking up the switchbacks that led hikers south along the PCT.

The hills behind his house had kept Mahmoud in shape and he was young, but his companions soon needed to stop for a break.

"What was that?" one of the men asked in Arabic. "Behind us." They had seen warning signs for grizzly bears. The northern part of the trail was the only section where grizzlies still lived.

"I hear nothing," answered Salem. He laughed. "Don't be spooked just because the trees are tall."

A dog's bark turned their heads back around. Aimless and his dog, Mutt, were on their return trip to Oregon. Mutt had seen something to chase and run ahead of his owner. The dog stopped when he reached the men. He growled.

Mahmoud smiled at the dog, but another Brigade member hissed, "Dog dinner!"

Mutt took off into the woods.

Aimless caught up as the men were pulling on their packs. "Hi, you seen a brown dog?"

Salem replied, "No, no dog."

Aimless noticed their clothes. Blue jeans, sneakers, T-shirts, and large backpacks. And all of them were smoking. Heavy packs with street clothes! Even day hikers wore loose clothing. And cigarettes? Hadn't they heard and seen warnings about the danger of smoking in this dry season?

"No, no dog," the man repeated.

"Well, thanks," said Aimless. "I'll wait here for a bit. Maybe he'll be back."

The man shrugged and put on his pack. He dropped the cigarette on the path, barely stepping on it. They turned south.

Mutt returned in a few minutes.

"Where you been, Mutt?" said Aimless. "Stay close to me."

Something wasn't right about the hikers he'd just met. He suddenly recalled smelling burned ashes as he passed the monument. Did these guys have something to do with that? Aimless decided to retrace the three miles back to Monument 78.

A group of hikers stood around a smoldering spot on the ground.

"Some asshole burned all of the notes," one hiker exclaimed.

"Jerk," another one said.

Aimless returned to the trail. Without identification, he didn't want to alert Canadian authorities. He remembered the forest ranger at Harts Pass. He'd spoken to her on his way north. When he reached the Pass this time, he'd tell her about the men. It wasn't a big deal to him, but maybe someone ought to know idiots are burning paper in the woods.

Aimless slowed his pace and kept Mutt in sight the rest of the afternoon. As he set up camp that evening, he whistled to Mutt who had wandered away again. He always shared his food with the dog, and that night he had an especially tempting dinner which he'd solicited from tourists in Manning before his return trip.

Instead of seeing Mutt run into the site, Aimless was startled by the Arab who'd spoken to him earlier that day. He was holding a bottle.

"Water?" he asked.

"Oh, hey," answered Aimless. "Sure, I got water."

There were plenty of streams around, Aimless knew, so why was this guy asking him for water? Maybe he didn't have a filter. Whatever, he wasn't going to question it.

He reached for his pack that held a bottle of water. He heard Mutt growl but never saw the knife.

TWENTY-EIGHT

NOTHER FIVE MILES and they'd be at Rainy Pass. This section of the trail climbed steadily through a mix of forest and high, thick brush, and hardly a mile passed that didn't involve crossing a fast-moving creek either on—or off—a bridge. Scenes of the Suiattle River flicked through Luke's mind. Even though the creeks on this stretch of the PCT were much smaller than the churning Suiattle, he found himself balking when the bridge was only a log or set of stones.

Other than his slow traversing of water, he was pleased he'd been able to keep up with Mike during the day's hike from Stehekin. Without the complication of Naomi and the turmoil she had a way of creating in him, he'd again focused on the basics of hiking, things he knew how to handle, like terrain and pace. He was back in his element—the woods, alert to any sign of unusual activity, free to make sense of it.

At the ranch he'd told Mike about rescuing Naomi from the Suiattle, but stopped the story there. Mike had listened, but hadn't responded other than to ask for more details about the river, which had been lower when he'd crossed it a week earlier. The conversation had turned to other tales of rescue. The ex-SEAL had plenty of those. Late into the night, Mike had regaled him with stories of rescuing hostages from pirates in Somalia. Luke easily imagined his ex-commando friend sliding down a rope from a helicopter in the middle of the night, slipping unseen into an enemy compound, doing whatever was necessary to accomplish the mission. He felt lucky to have a guy along with this level of experience.

The muscular sound of cascading water brought Luke to a halt. *Not another one.* This time, a narrow, mossy log offered the only dry passage to the other side. Mike trotted across as deftly as a fox. Luke glared at him and then began an unsteady journey, arms outstretched, clutching his trekking poles.

"You look like a giant insect," said Mike, laughing.

"I've had enough of those," replied Luke, back on solid ground.

"At least it's not raining. And we're nearly to Rainy Pass."

Luke groaned at the joke. "Yeah. And the weather report looks good for the next few days." He tightened his waist strap. "A big break for us, more than one day without rain, or up here in the Cascades, snow."

"You ever thought about special ops?" Mike asked, continuing up the trail. "You can obviously handle yourself and seem pretty savvy in the bush—other than crossing creeks."

"Nope. Can't climb ropes. Never could. Not enough upper body I guess." Luke chuckled. "I actually tried out for the FBI Hostage Rescue Team early in my career. Didn't go too well."

Mike stopped and looked back over his shoulder, surprise on his face. "Is that right?"

"Scored at the top in orienteering, shooting, and endurance, stuff like running hills, but bottomed out at climbing ropes. Failed the pull-ups and platform climbs, too. They basically laughed at me and sent me on my way."

"Yeah, well they're pretty stuck on their physical prowess and don't take other strengths into account. It's quite a macho culture."

"Like the SEALs?"

"Yeah, I suppose so," said Mike. "Sometimes, anyway." He shifted his pack. "These guns are getting heavy."

Luke nodded in agreement. He decided not to explain his loathing of guns, especially after Mike's praise of Glocks. That was probably another reason the HRT had thrown him out. He hadn't shown an appropriate admiration of the guns he'd had to shoot.

In a half hour they left the forest and crossed Route 20 into the parking lot at Rainy Pass. The pass was a popular stop for thru-hikers, and trail angels often stayed for a few days, stocked with food and drink. This evening was no different. Lanterns lit the area. To the side, a variety of tents stippled the woods. Makeshift seats from coolers and logs ringed a crackling bonfire. Hikers were sitting around the fire drinking, eating, and exchanging stories. They were a ratty-looking bunch, some with dreadlocks sticking out from under Alpaca hats, others with shaved heads, and still others with so much beard their faces were all but hidden. An assortment of tattoos and piercings made the scene look almost like a tribal gathering.

In fact, as they walked up to the group, Luke wasn't sure if the men they were to meet were there. It didn't look like it. Luke and Mike raised their hands in greeting, but continued past to find a decent campsite.

"Doesn't seem like any law enforcement types are here," commented Luke as they finished pitching their tents. "Only the usual collection."

"Could be," agreed Mike. "Let's set up our tents and check out the ring-around-the-bonfire."

They returned to the spirited group, and it wasn't long before they were giving out their trail names. One hiker offered them a couple of beers. "Courtesy of Angel Adams," he said, pointing to a middle-aged man talking to a couple of other people.

"Hey, Angel," the hiker said, "Sea Dog and Camper."

Angel walked over. "Good to meet you," he said shaking hands firmly.

Angel was tall, and his graying hair and unshaven face lent him a grizzled, unkempt look. At odds were his dark, piercing eyes. Luke had an idea Angel knew exactly who he and Mike were.

"Like you to meet a couple more guys," Angel said, leading them to the edge of the bonfire. Two men, dressed in boots and lightweight clothing, stood drinking coffee. "This here is Steve and Lewis."

Lewis, the shorter of the two, looked half Japanese. His long black hair was pulled into a pony tail, and it didn't appear as if he ever smiled. He shook hands with Luke and Mike but said nothing.

Steve was friendlier. "Heard about you," he said to Mike. He was solidly built and moved with ease and confidence.

"You, too," he turned to Luke. "Glad we can come along. And Leon sends his best."

"We all got some vacation coming to us, so we thought we'd do a little hiking with you," added Angel. "Leon arranged it. He said we might do some hunting, too. Doesn't matter if we catch anything or not."

"Thanks," said Luke. He motioned to their campsite. "We pitched our tents over there."

"Ours aren't far," said Steve.

Luke nodded. "Okay. Let's get an early start, say 5 A.M. We can talk more up the trail when we're alone."

"Sounds good," said Angel.

The five men finished their drinks and headed to their tents.

Luke wormed into his sleeping bag. He was tired but not able to close his eyes. He regarded the tent's ceiling. *So this is the team Charlie and Ken put together. They look committed and like they can take care of themselves.* He turned over on his side. *Three of them, plus Mike and myself. Five guys against who-knows-what. Maybe nothing. So be it.*

TWENTY-NINE

THE SMALL CONFERENCE ROOM adjacent to Jennifer Johnson's office was crowded. Jen, a fit 50-year-old with fading red hair pulled up into a twist, sat at one end of an oval table. Her tan two-piece suit buckled across her large chest. She was reading intently through several documents and looked up briefly when Bill Scully and Dirk Barnstable entered. They took the two empty chairs. Charlie Logan and Terri Densmore were already seated.

Jen pushed the report forward and looked around the table. She was not smiling. "What's going on here?" she asked Bill. "Why wasn't I notified about this sooner? I've just had a rather difficult phone conversation with Carol Linderman over at Justice."

Bill wished he could answer that she hadn't wanted to be bothered when she had a big golf tournament to attend, but instead he said, "At the time, there weren't enough specifics about a possible threat. We had pieces, but nothing to connect the dots." He pointed to one of the folders on the table. "Nothing until now."

Bill was referring to the newest intel coming from the Pakistani government via the Terrorist Threat Center in Washington. Pakistani commandos had raided a radical Islamic camp in the mountains near the border between Pakistan and Afghanistan and captured a high-level operations commander. Under questioning, he had handed over complete plans for blowing up a dirty bomb somewhere on the West Coast of the United States. U.S. intelligence wanted to know what larger organization ran this camp. They asked the Pakistanis if they could interrogate the commander but were told that the prisoner was no longer available. They all knew what that meant. The dirty material, according to the plans, was coming through Vancouver across an isolated border in British Columbia. Terri had rushed the report to Charlie and Dirk, and they had brought it to Bill.

When he'd scanned the document, Bill had abruptly taken his shoes off his desk. The threat was real—and he hadn't acted on the earlier intelligence Charlie and Terri had brought to his attention. This time there was no indecision.

A sense of panic began to rise in the conference room. Jen had no intention of taking the blame for her office not responding to a potential terrorist threat. Even worse, she was suddenly the focus of what could prove to be a national crisis. With little experience in counterterrorism, this was much more than she had bargained for as the special agent in charge of the L.A. office. Jen realized she was entirely unprepared for what to do next.

The room was silent. Four pairs of eyes watched her. She kept her own eyes focused on the folders lying on the table, moving her lips, but saying nothing.

Charlie recognized her mortification. He spoke quietly. "We need to move, Jen. You've got to contact headquarters. The Center's information on the threat probably hasn't reached them yet. They'll tell us what else they need. Quick, make the call."

Jen lifted her head. The agents—her agents—sat upright, unmoving, waiting for her to tell them what to do. But how could she? She'd flattered and charmed her way from a street agent to a supervisor and finally to one of the top management positions in the FBI. And she'd always relied on competent people around her. Had never needed to be competent herself. That's how the system had worked for her.

She knew she wasn't stupid. She'd done very well at the FBI Academy, even handled the infamous shotgun. It's just that playing the role of a pretty woman had been so easy, much easier than being an accountable and responsible agent. She was amazed at how simple it had been and had let it happen.

Her throat tightened as if it were in a vice. She felt like she might pass out. Then she remembered Paul. Paul from the New Haven office. He'd help her. He had to. Her mouth formed a thin line. "Okay. I'll do that."

Charlie and Terri were then excused.

In the hallway, Terri looked at Charlie. "Unbelievable," she said.

The door opened. "Can you come back in for a minute, Charlie?"

He returned to the table, but remained standing.

"Before I make that call," said Jen, "I just want to know. How did Luke Chamberlin find out about this? And, how did he put together some rogue posse? Anybody have any ideas?"

Bill said nothing. Dirk shrugged his shoulders.

"Luke heard from an old Soviet adversary. They became friends of a sort after Luke caught and arrested him in New York," Charlie finally said. All three agents turned to him. "This ex-spy told Luke that stolen radioactive material could potentially be brought to the U.S., but he didn't know where."

Charlie looked directly at Jen. "I knew we wouldn't react, or take the time to even investigate a little, since the information was vague—and coming from Luke. I asked Leon Malone to make preliminary inquiries. That was it."

Jen stared hard at Charlie. Her jaw was set. "All of this running around from information that originated from an ex-Soviet spy? And coming through Luke Chamberlin?"

Bill and Dirk looked down at the table.

"The call, Jen," said Charlie, "make the call."

"I'll deal with you later," she responded. She picked up the intelligence report on her desk and turned to the men. "You can all go now," she said. "I'll get back to you about our next steps. Meanwhile, find Luke and his yahoos and get them off the case. If you have to, bring that loon in on a material witness warrant. I don't need this stuff to happen at this point in my career."

Jen left the conference room and closed the door to her office. *Luke Chamberlin. How the hell did he get involved? Hadn't he disappeared into the woods somewhere?* Jen opened her safe and took out a key that fit into a lock on the side of a phone on her desk. When a light came on, she picked up the receiver and punched in the number for Paul McLarney, the agent in charge of counterterrorism at FBI Headquarters. She waited while Paul did the same at his end to access the secure voice line.

"Paul," she said when a voice answered. "This is Jen Johnson. We've got a possible situation here. We've got to act now." Her voice caught. "And I really don't know what to do."

Jen knew Paul well. She'd been an agent on his squad in New Haven, CT, before he left for Quantico to help train new agents. Their affair had been brief but intense. He never told his family. He owed her.

She summarized the briefing she'd just had in her conference room.

"Holy shit," said Paul when Jen had finished. "Send me everything you know in a secure email. Now!"

"It should be there in a few minutes." She lowered her voice. "And Paul, thanks."

"Yeah, right. I'll get back to you."

Paul told his secretary to expect a secure email with attached .pdf documents. Then he reached for the antacid tablets he kept in his drawer. He'd recently arrived at Headquarters from Quantico, where he'd been non-operational, lecturing new agents on international affairs. Like Jen, he wasn't sure what to do next. The burrito he'd eaten for lunch lurched in his stomach.

Once the report was in his hands, Paul did the only thing he could think of. He called the director's office.

Director Mayberry slammed the phone down and snapped orders. A protocol was immediately set in motion, headed by the Rapid Deployment Team from Quantico, VA. Their first priority was to establish a command post. They pulled out satellite and topographic maps and found several likely egress routes near the border between British Columbia and Washington. One of the team members pointed to Mazama, a small town near these areas. Outside the town stood an old smoke jumper and fire fighting station large enough to handle helicopters. An abandoned World War II airfield a few miles farther away could accommodate cargo planes. The team chose the Mazama Forest Ranger Station as the command post from which operational teams would spread into the more remote areas. Assisting the Rapid Deployment Team were the FBI's Hostage Rescue Team and the Nuclear Emergency Support Team who would search for the terrorists and any possible radioactive material they might be transporting.

Within 12 hours of Jen's call to FBI headquarters, the Mazama command post was operational. Once Jen heard it was done, she ordered Bill to handle their end of the situation. She locked the door to her office and picked up the phone. She'd had enough of this crap. A golf tournament wasn't far enough away. She called the Career Board at Headquarters and asked for immediate transfer back to Washington—where she'd be safe.

THIRTY

ACH OF THE FIVE MEN knew how to quickly and quietly break camp. They were gone from Rainy Pass before the birds stirred. They hiked along the forested trail, their steps sure and smooth. After several miles, the men stopped for water and a brief breakfast of power bars.

Luke started. "I've put together all the intel from my contacts at the FBI and information they've received from the Canadian intelligence services. From what we can tell, dirty bomb material may be moving from Canada into the U.S. Terrorists are probably responsible, though we're not sure who they are—if they have ties to radical Islamic groups, or if they're a small pop-up cell, or homegrown malcontents. We know the material was likely bought in Russia, then sold through the black market to a militant group who transported it through Pakistan, over to the Philippines and across the Pacific to Vancouver. I don't know where they intend to take it, but L.A. is a likely spot. They tried once in 2000 to bring a bomb down to California, and it's logical that they'll try again. Remember the World Trade Centers. The second attack brought them down."

None of the men said anything.

Luke continued. "The last piece of intel I got in Stehekin mentioned something about a remote spot on the border between British Columbia and the U.S. There's a lot of territory where terrorists could cross, but they'll need some sort of access. We've got about 90 miles to Monument 78 at the border. That's one accessible spot, but there are lots of others. We'll get up there and keep our eyes and ears open, and maybe we'll have something to share with the RCMP."

He surveyed the small group. "We're going to stay flexible in our plans, because we have no idea what sort of activity we might encounter, if any. That's it."

"Let's introduce ourselves quickly," he added, "and then get moving. I guess you already know who Mike and I are. How about you?" He faced Angel.

"Angel Adams, detective with the Washington County sheriff's department on detail with the JTTF. I work narcotics. I like to hike."

Steve spoke next. "Steve Rawlinson. I'm a detective, too. Also with the JTTF in Washington County. I'm divorced. Lost a son in Afghanistan."

"I'm a forest ranger with the National Forest Service," said Lewis. "I worked 10 years as a Coast Guard sharpshooter. Sat in a helicopter and shot up engines of fleeing drug boats. I got sick of the ocean, so I left the Coast Guard and got a job with the National Forest Service. I'm a decent shot."

"Speaking of which, I'm tired of lugging these around," said Mike, handing out the Glocks and magazines. "You never know."

Lewis refused the gun, pointing to a long case attached to his pack.

"Here's a little more weight," Steve added. He passed around handheld radios. "In the event we get separated. Cell phones sometimes don't work so well up here, and these have a 20-mile range."

"Seems like you all know what you're doing," said Luke, nodding his approval. "Let's put in some miles."

⊛　⊛　⊛

A DAY LATER, THE UNORTHODOX TEAM APPROACHED Harts Pass. It was late morning, and though the sun shone, it was cool, and lingering fog coated the men's faces with a damp sheen. Mike was in the lead, with Lewis just behind, and then Steve and Angel. Luke decided to stay at the back. That way he'd have a better grasp of the situation, both human and otherwise. He walked lightly, wishing, at that moment, he wore moccasins. They were tough, yet soft enough to avoid making noise. And you could feel the terrain through them, test it with your toes. He'd always worn moccasins when he hunted with Granddad.

⊛　⊛　⊛

"Stealth," Granddad said, "is a necessity, not only to hunt, but to become part of the spirit that is the woods."

Luke had had to learn stealth the hard way. "I can't do it, Granddad," he'd said as a teen hunting one fall with his grandfather. "I still make noise no matter how many times I try." He kicked the leaves in disgust. "These moccasins don't work."

Granddad replied, "Try again. Be more patient with your feet. You are Amik, the beaver, but when you hunt, move like your cat. Think how Smoky places her feet to avoid making noise." He used his hands to mimic the walk of Luke's cat.

＊　＊　＊

AFTER MANY NIGHTS of eating berries and mushrooms, he had finally learned. With the soles of his feet and his toes, he could discern between roots of different trees, between acorns and stones, between seeds and pebbles.

Luke breathed deeply through his nose and listened closely, allowing his senses to channel information from the air, ground, and vegetation that his eyes couldn't receive. Useful information. A slight whiff of smoke caught his attention. "Smoke, Mike, from a recent fire."

Mike nodded. He motioned for the team to slow down. It was quiet. Too quiet, he thought, even at a remote pass 6,000 feet above sea level. They glimpsed the guardhouse 200 yards ahead. The front door was wide open, the screen door swinging on its hinges. Odd on such a cool day. And where did the smoke come from?

Luke felt a familiar pang in his stomach.

"Shhh," said Mike, holding up his hand.

They heard the mewing of a cat.

Mike turned to the team. "How 'bout two of us go up there, and the rest wait here," he said, motioning to Lewis.

Lewis nodded. He and Mike picked their way slowly to the guardhouse.

Steve, Angel, and Luke waited in a silent edginess. Around them, charred trees, shrubs, and grass poked through the dry, rocky soil. Boot prints provided the only sign of life. Luke squatted close to the trail to get a better look at them. He recognized a set, one with an imprint from the toe and heel of a light boot, cut in half by a smooth band, likely by duct tape. It was an unmistakable signature track. An uneasiness gripped him.

Luke's radio crackled. He clicked it on. "Get up here," said Mike, "at the back door. It's the ranger. She's dead. And it's not nice."

The three men walked quickly to the guardhouse. Slumped across the threshold of the back door was Mary Lou's body. Her head rested a few feet away.

They gaped at the bloody scene.

"She's been dead maybe a couple of hours," said Mike.

"This changes things," said Steve.

"Someone is sending a signal," continued Mike. "I don't know where they're from, but they're clearly on a mission. Whoever did this must have panicked for some reason, enough to murder an innocent woman. I'd say they're real close."

"What do you say, Luke?"

The uneasiness Luke had felt mushroomed into unbridled alarm. Luke nodded slowly. "These are the guys, the ones with a dirty bomb. It couldn't be anyone else. Not to do this. I agree. They panicked. Didn't want the ranger to get in the way. That means either they're waiting for a signal to move, or they're meeting up with another cell."

"I'm going to look around a bit," said Lewis. He turned to retrace his steps to the front of the house.

"I'll go with you," said Steve.

"We'll need to leave the body as is," said Angel. "Crime on federal property now."

Luke took off his pack and crouched down.

"What is it, Luke?" asked Mike.

"Not sure. Looks like there was quite a scuffle here. Maybe the ranger put up a fight."

He peered at the dirt around the back step of the guardhouse. Drag marks crisscrossed the area. He touched a couple of rocks. They had left small marks in the dirt where they'd been rolled over. There was blood everywhere and several types of boot prints, including those he had dreaded to find.

Mike and Angel joined Luke. "Interesting print," Mike said, pointing to the track. He looked directly at Luke.

"It's Naomi's," Luke admitted.

"You think she got mixed up in all of this?"

"I don't know," answered Luke, standing up. Shrubs grew in back of the guardhouse, and he inspected them closely. Several twigs were bent. Leaves were scattered underneath, and drops of blood dotted the grass. A small pile of rocks hastily placed, marked a spot. A shiver ran down his spine. What had happened to Naomi?

"Who's Naomi?" asked Angel.

"A lady hiker Luke met in Oregon," replied Mike. "She was a day or so ahead of us."

Steve came back around. "Hey," he said softly, "Lewis sees them. They're about a quarter mile away at a campsite."

Mike drew in a breath and looked around at the others. "We've got to do something about these guys." He turned to Luke. "That's what we—what you—intended. Naomi will have to wait."

Luke spoke so only Mike heard. "I can't leave her, Mike."

"Yeah, you can, Luke. Think what's at stake here. If these guys do have dirty stuff. Just think. We need to check it out."

Luke slowly stood up. Everything suddenly went out of focus. For so many miles, he'd been sure that if the threat did exist, it was centered farther north, not here, not at Harts Pass. And not when Naomi had passed through.

They followed Steve to the front of the guardhouse, where Lewis had set up his gear, a .308 Remington lightweight tactical rifle, with a Leupold 4.5 to 14 power, and a 50 mm scope fitted with tactical knobs for fast, accurate adjustment. The rifle rested on its folding bi-pod, attached to the front of the stock at a spot where Lewis had an unobstructed view. Using the scope, he had scanned the area around Harts Pass. He motioned for the rest of the team to come over.

Next to the rifle lay what looked like an iPhone.

"Nice piece," said Mike, motioning to the rifle. "What's the iPhone for?"

"Comes with a sniper app," answered Lewis, "to calculate wind speed and bullet drop. Lucky thing service up here is good."

"Who knew," muttered Angel.

Lewis pointed to a distant campsite, about 400 yards away. "These guys are busy, packing up, maybe," said Lewis, hardly audible. Then he positioned the scope and motioned for Luke to look through it.

The scope's crosshairs magnified the campsite. Men were milling around old military-style tents. A run-down truck was parked to the side. Several of the men had dark hair and beards. One was a young man, a boy really. Another had red hair, and on his head sat a forest ranger's cap, askew. Luke jerked his head back. Lewis nodded and then put his finger to his lips. He motioned for the others to look.

When they'd all viewed the campsite, Mike led the team back to the guardhouse. "It looks like they're getting ready to leave. We don't want to lose them if they're carrying a dirty bomb."

"Don't want to lose them?" The question came from Steve. He turned to Luke. "This was supposed to be reconnaissance. We were to report what we saw—remember?"

"Looks like I was wrong," said Luke. "I'm as surprised as you, Steve. Problem is, we're out of time. Mike is right. They look like they're leaving."

"And no one here but us," said Angel.

Lewis put a stick of gum in his mouth.

"There's five of them, five of us," Mike continued. "I'd prefer a 2:1 ratio, good to bad, but we'll have to make do." He stared hard at the men. "Any problems with this? Everyone okay with what we've got to do?"

Each man nodded. If there had been doubt earlier, it wasn't in evidence anymore.

"How's that for a look-out spot, Lewis?" he asked.

"Fine."

"Can you take out one target, clean?"

"No problem."

"I'll let you know when. Meanwhile, the rest of us will stay more or less together. We don't want any confusion between us and them. We'll approach the campsite and capture or eliminate whatever tries to crawl away. We'll see how that goes."

"Guess we'll be hunting after all," said Angel.

The men took the Glocks from their packs. The guns were already loaded with a magazine and each man carried an extra. Mike watched the team members smoothly pull the slide chambering a round and tuck the guns into holsters that fit around their thighs. Only Luke seemed a little slow moving his hand around the gun. He had placed it into his holster but spent a lot more time adjusting the tomahawk tied to his belt.

"What are you going to do with that tomahawk, Luke?" asked Angel. "A gun's a lot faster and more accurate."

"Maybe," Luke replied.

When they were ready, the men hid their packs in shrubs near the guardhouse. Steve scooped up the cat and put her inside.

Lewis returned to his rifle, sitting calmly, chewing gum.

"No talking on the radios unless we have to," said Mike.

He turned to Luke. "You ready?"

"Yeah," replied Luke. "Let's do this."

THIRTY-ONE

THE MAYOR OF MAZAMA had cancelled the old-time fiddling contest scheduled for the upcoming week. She told restaurants and cafés to order more food, the inns and motels to find cots. Teams and special forces from both the United States and Canada had invaded her town.

The tiny, quiet ranger station at the edge of Mazama had been transformed into a bustling incident command center filled with people, computers, and gear. Running the operation was the Hostage Rescue Team's Glen Fields. Before joining the FBI, Fields had fought in the first Gulf War. Dressed in black Ninja clothing, he cut a serious and capable figure. All morning, he'd been on the phone and looking at maps, planning to send teams to any area accessible to terrorists. He conferred with a small group of men around a map spread out on a large table. He pointed to several spots along the border between Canada and the U.S. A quarter mile away, the abandoned airstrip, used now to launch heli-skiers, was lined with planes and helicopters, awaiting orders to move out.

The station's head ranger had been waiting patiently to speak with Fields. With some exasperation, Fields finally spoke to him.

"I'm Chet Lawson, assigned to this station," the ranger began, ignoring Fields' obvious impatience. "I don't know if this might help your investigation," he said, "but a ranger at our guardhouse at Harts Pass called here a couple of days ago. She makes a routine call every day to let us know if she needs supplies or anything."

"What's your point," demanded Fields.

"Well, it's just odd. She never misses a day. She didn't call this morning. And that call two days ago? She said that three men were at a burned-out campsite near the pass. Men, who in her opinion, weren't hikers or campers. She felt they might be up to no good, as she put it. Obviously she felt worried enough to note it."

The information caught Fields' attention. "How could she be positive the people weren't hikers or campers?"

"I'm not sure," replied Lawson, "but Mary Lou is one of our best interns. She's very thorough and precise. She includes the smallest details in her reports. In this case, she mentioned that the men had been there a few weeks ago, looking for the hawks, which don't migrate for another couple of weeks. She also asked if hawks migrate at night, because these men had night goggles. Fancy ones."

"Night goggles?"

Lawson nodded. "Only, hawks don't migrate at night."

An alarm sounded in Fields' head, loud and clear. "Hawks don't migrate at night?"

"No, sir, they don't."

Fields turned to the map. "Where is this pass?"

Lawson pointed to it. "It's 26 miles from here, up a bad dirt road. In fact, I've got crews on the road now trying to clean it up. A rock slide at Dead Horse Point has made it impassable. It'll be another day before vehicles can get by."

"It won't take us that long to clear it out," said Fields. "Stay here, will you?"

He turned to one of his men. "We need to go here, to Harts Pass." He poked the map. "The road's blocked. Let's get a team ready to do some rock rolling. I want some men and heavy equipment—STAT."

THIRTY-TWO

HARTS PASS, WA;

SEPTEMBER 13

WITH LITTLE COVER left from the old forest fires, Luke's team took almost an hour to approach the terrorist campsite. They moved down the hillside as a single unit with Mike in the middle, Luke to his left, and Steve and Angel to his right.

Fanning out thinly, each man followed a slightly different route, moving slowly and cautiously, and always within sight of each other. Luke let himself cross the terrain automatically. He was thankful not to have to concentrate. His mind wasn't on the mission. It was on the small pile of rocks behind the guardhouse.

When they were nearly in position, he called Mike on his radio. "I'm going for Naomi," he said softly. "Start without me. I'll be right back."

"No, Luke!" whispered Mike. "Stay in position."

He searched frantically for Luke in the scrub to his left, but he had disappeared.

LUKE CIRCLED BACK to the guardhouse. *Thank God, no hikers,* he thought. He wondered if that might have something to do with federal agents finally arriving and stopping people from using roads and trails. He hoped so.

While they were making their way toward the campsite, Luke had weighed the situation. Leaving his team was completely against his training and his nature. But the pile of rocks and what they represented—a clear plea for help—was too strong a call. He simply had to find Naomi, no matter in what condition. She wouldn't have gotten far, and Mike and the others could handle the situation until he got back. At least he was counting on that.

He crouched near the rocks behind the guardhouse. From this point, he began to cut sign—to analyze physical evidence of Naomi. Ahead, boot prints marked the ground erratically. Naomi's signature prints were among them and led away from the site. So did blood. He started to follow the clear track. But then the trail met rock and stopped. Not even a drop of blood.

He turned to aerial sign—the light undersides of bent leaves, bruising, broken twigs. These were precious indications of Naomi's movement and direction. He smelled a broken twig. The break was fresh. She wasn't far ahead. Rock changed back to dirt. More boot prints and small pebbles kicked aside. Blood again.

Luke heard a gunshot. He cringed.

He kept going. He concentrated only on reading the sign, the clues to Naomi's whereabouts. A strand of her hair hanging from the branch of a shrub bent in the breeze. She was near. He sensed her. He quickened his pace.

Under a shrub, a shirt and pair of pants lay flat on the ground, arranged as they would look on a person. There wasn't a body there, or anywhere nearby. Luke touched the shirt. The clothes belonged to Naomi, he was sure of that. But where was she? He studied the splatters of blood that stained the edges of the shirt sleeve. If she'd been wounded, why was blood only on the sleeves?

He sat back on his heels and rubbed his forehead. Thoughts spun around in his head. None of this made any sense. He fixed his eyes on the clothes again. His stomach suddenly knotted, and a feeling of disbelief washed over him.

He ran back toward the campsite, praying his gut was wrong.

THIRTY-THREE

WHEN THEY WERE in position, Mike spoke softly into his radio. Lewis was on his stomach looking into the scope. Using a handheld Kestrel Model 4000 weather station and range finder, he calculated wind speed and direction to the target. He inputted the information into his iPhone sniper app, which calculated the adjustments he'd need to make to the rifle scope. He turned several knobs on the rifle. The Mil Dot retical of the scope moved from one potential target to another. Lewis lined up a shot and stopped chewing his gum. He carefully controlled his breathing as his finger gradually increased pressure on the trigger of the rifle. The 250 grain bullet left the barrel of the rifle in less than a second, and one of Mahmoud's hiking companions dropped to the ground, a hole blown open in his chest.

Mike watched from his perch. He whistled under his breath. He'd never make fun of another forest ranger again.

When the Brigade saw their companion fall, they scattered, not knowing where the shot had originated, or from what direction. Two of the men ran into the tent, two others dove behind fallen trees.

One charged back out from the tent waving a small Stechkin APS 9 mm pistol. He shouted at his companions in Arabic, urging them to follow. He chanted "Allah Akbar! Allah Akbar!" "God is great! God is great!" Without caution or thought, he crawled through blackened logs and shrub behind the campsite.

"Hey," said Angel, stepping out from behind a tree.

The Brigade member swung around just in time to take a bullet from the Glock.

Lewis watched through his scope.

There was no more movement in the campsite. The team waited. Perfectly silent.

A half hour passed. Where was Luke? Mike motioned for them to start down into the campsite. He had waited long enough for Luke. Fuck Luke. He liked the odds better now anyway.

Lewis stayed put.

Angel swung farther to the right of the campsite, staying in dense shrubs.

Steve continued down straight.

Mike made his way carefully, keeping low to the ground. He scuttled through a cover of boulders, then slowly stood. He looked straight into the barrel of a gun.

"Oh shit," he muttered. It was the young kid, the one with the knit cap. Mike swerved away, but not in time. The bullet tore through the back of his right arm. He doubled over, clutching his arm. The Glock fell to the ground.

Mahmoud took a couple of steps closer. He pointed the gun at Mike's head, his hand shaking. He opened and closed his mouth.

Understanding what was to come, Mike stood still and breathed calmly. A movement caught his attention. His eyes flicked slightly to the right. Something rose from behind a bush about 60 yards away. Mike couldn't make it out. It didn't look like a person, more like a shadow. The image moved, then stopped.

A blur somersaulted through the air. Mike's eyes widened imperceptibly. He heard a thin hum, then a thunk. Mahmoud took a step forward. He looked up at the sky, mouthing "ambri," "mother." Then he fell. Luke's tomahawk had sunk deep into Mahmoud's spine.

Mike was still staring at Mahmoud when Luke reached him.

"You alright, Mike?" Luke asked.

"Yeah, just a flesh wound. The boy was so scared he couldn't hold the gun straight. Lucky for me."

Luke touched the boy's neck, then pulled his tomahawk from his back.

"Jesus, Luke, how the hell do you know how to do that? From that distance? I didn't even see you."

"Granddad, Mike. Plus, I don't like guns." Luke shrugged.

"You sure you're okay?"

"You don't like guns? You're telling me this now?"

Mike looked at Mahmoud's body, then back at Luke.

"Mike, we've got to get to the others, quick." He helped Mike to his feet.

"I tracked Naomi…"

"Stupid move," interrupted Mike.

"I know, I know, but Mike, she wasn't there. Only a set of empty clothes. Blood spattered on the shirt sleeves but nowhere else. Something's very, very wrong."

Mike stopped. "A set of bloody clothes but no body?"

Luke nodded.

"Luke, are you thinking what I am?"

"I don't know. I don't know what to think."

"What's the gut know?"

"Not good, Mike."

They skirted back and found Angel and Steve near the tents. They were bent over the body of another Brigade member. Steve was wiping blood off a knife.

"This guy is a westerner. We tried to talk him into surrendering, but he didn't want to," said Steve. "You okay, Mike?"

"He took one in the arm, but he'll be alright," answered Luke. "I got the shooter. It was the kid."

"I didn't hear another shot," said Angel.

"I didn't use a gun," replied Luke.

Steve's eyebrows raised slightly. "That's four of them," he said. "Where's the fifth?"

"You check inside the tent?"

"Yeah, we looked around. Nothing there."

Luke felt his radio vibrate on his hip. He clicked it on. "Asshole in the bushes, to your right," whispered Lewis. "He doesn't have a gun and he doesn't know I'm looking at him. Lure him out."

Luke peered to the right of the campsite. He examined the ground, then a clump of brush. "Got him," he said, tilting his head toward the bushes. He unbuckled his tomahawk, estimating the distance. The brush wouldn't allow a clean throw.

"Let's give Lewis a clear shot," he said, putting the tomahawk back into its sheath. "Start to rummage around the site. He'll come after us."

The three men turned to the tents, their backs to the hiding Brigade member.

Salem sprinted from the bushes, a knife raised. The shot from Lewis' rifle hit him in the back, exploding his rib cage, and he dropped as if his legs had been cut out from under him. He made a soft gurgling noise as blood poured from the chest wound. Then he was still.

"He knew he was going to die," said Steve, standing over the body. "It was like he wanted to."

"I'll radio Lewis," said Angel.

While they waited for Lewis to join them, Steve cleaned Mike's wound. Luke and Angel checked inside the tents.

"They must have been in real hurry to leave," Angel said, entering one. It was a mess, clothes and gear strewn around, cots turned over.

"Be careful what you touch," Luke said, squatting beside a cot. From under it, he pulled clothes and some small, wrinkled papers covered with hand-written notes. He smoothed them out and examined them. Although neatly printed, the notes were disjointed, first a phrase or two, then blank spaces, then a crossed-out line.

Glancing down the lines, he spotted the acronym, LEO, several times. LEO stood for law enforcement officer and could mean anyone from a local sheriff to an FBI agent. He read closely.

"Met a LEO today. Retired. Not likely a threat."

Then more phrases about trail conditions, numbers of hikers, the weather.

Then lines crossed out.

Then, "LEO not staying long at Cascade Locks."

More scratched-out lines. Luke couldn't read them. He smoothed out the next ball of paper.

"LEO moving at a good pace. No problem keeping up."

The last legible line read: "LEO moving fast towards pass."

With a wrench in his gut, Luke realized the notes were written by Naomi. About him. About his movements on the trail, his pace, his stops. The notes were an assessment of his threat to the mission. *Naomi. Who are you?* He shook his head back and forth. *One of them? You can't be.*

Luke stood up, the papers bunched in his hand.

"What are those?" asked Mike, walking in.

"These are Naomi's notes. She's one of them, Mike. She wrote notes to report to this terrorist cell about hikers' movements and trail conditions, the weather—whatever could help them. I was one of her persons of interest." He pushed the notes toward Mike.

"She's not here now. Must have escaped when things got noisy," said Mike. "She probably decided she'd be more useful alive, maybe to help with a future mission. Can we track her?"

"I doubt it. Naomi knew this area pretty well. She's long gone." Luke crumpled the notes in his fist. "She's also pretty good at diversion. Look at the blood and empty set of clothes she left for me. She knew I'd track her."

"She was leading you away from the campsite, Luke," said Mike. "Don't you see? She didn't want you there. And, she was telling you she was gone."

Luke looked away from his friend. "How could I not have seen through her? I should have known."

"You didn't want to know," replied Mike. He laid his good hand on Luke's shoulder.

Angel poked his head into the tent. "Better get in the other tent, Luke. There's a backpack you need to look at."

He and Mike followed Angel into the second tent. In a corner lay a small backpack. Luke slowly undid the ties at the top. He motioned his teammates away. "Something is tightly wrapped in newspaper at the bottom. A box, maybe."

"Looks like we might have found gold," said Angel. "Let's call in some reinforcements. They won't want to miss this." He picked up his radio and left the tent.

Luke didn't touch the newspaper, but carefully lifted a copy of the Koran out of the pack. Inside the cover was a photo of a family. Mahmoud was standing next to his mother, father, brother, sister, in front of their shack. The area looked much like the hills around his own community in Southern California. Same dry, brown grass. Same sparse trees. Luke bowed his head and closed the book.

THIRTY-FOUR

THE AREA AROUND the guardhouse swarmed with federal agents, local police, Evidence Response Teams, crime scene investigators, and the media. They'd arrived an hour after Luke and his team had taken down the terrorists. Agents from the Nuclear Energy Support Team weren't far behind, and the dirty bomb material had been safely packaged and removed. Along with the bomb material, they'd found instructions concerning its movement into California and down to Los Angeles. There had been enough cesium 137 in the metal box at the bottom of Mahmoud's backpack to contaminate and disrupt a lot of Los Angeles, particularly if several bombs were detonated.

At first, Fields and the other HRT members were rough on Luke and his team, immediately handcuffing them. They took the Glocks and Lewis' rifle, asked for ID, and questioned them about why they were there, how they had gotten the intel, and how they had put it together.

Luke didn't offer much in the way of explanation. "I have nothing to say. It'll all be in a report from the L.A. FBI. You going to keep us in cuffs?"

Fields gave him a long, hard look. He knew that once the press arrived and found out this rogue posse had stopped terrorists en route to California with a box of cesium 137, they'd be heroes. They were heroes. It'd behoove him to act like it. Fields nodded and took off the cuffs. He shook Luke's hand.

"Fields," said Luke before he left, "you might want to think about tracking the terrorist who escaped. She's a woman named Naomi. She'll hide for a while, but probably won't disappear completely."

"I'll do that."

Luke turned from Fields and thanked the members of his team. They'd answer any remaining questions and Charlie and Ken would handle their end of the situation. Maybe they'd even get an award out of it. That left Gennady, whom he'd contact when he got home.

"I'll keep your phone number," he said to Mike.

"Good. I'm always up for a reconnoiter."

Luke cut behind the main part of Harts Pass and picked up the PCT heading north. The events of the past few days had drained him. He'd made some bad choices that could have led to good people losing their lives. But he'd also made some good choices, ones that reminded him of who he was. He tightened the straps of his pack for the 1,000th time. The only way he knew to deal with it all was to walk, toward Monument 78.

Sometimes the mountains in the northern Cascades said no. The accumulation of snow proved impossible for hikers to pass. He'd read that in a PCT hiker's journal. Not this day. Only a dusting lay beneath Luke's boots. This day the snowy peaks hailing him in the distance offered possibility. And Luke headed toward them.

. . .

A DOG'S BARK BROUGHT HIM out of the silence.

"Mutt," said Luke, petting the dog's head. "Where's Aimless?"

Mutt whined, then trotted up the trail, swiveling his head to see if Luke was following. In a quarter of a mile, Mutt stopped, sniffed the ground, then veered into the woods. Luke followed. Aimless' body had been dragged off the trail and covered with leaves. Mutt whined again and lay down.

"Christ. Not Aimless too." Luke took off his pack, his thoughts returning to the scene at the campsite, and then to Naomi. Who was she? How could she have been involved in such horrible acts? As a foolish follower? Or devoted terrorist of a yet uncovered cell? He didn't have answers to his troubling questions. And he wasn't going to look for them now. Not ever.

He bent over the young hiker. In the Chippewa tradition, he positioned Aimless' body so that his feet faced west. He had no birch bark for a covering, so instead, he used his tomahawk to peel strips of bark from larch trees. After he had placed the bark over the body, he lit a small fire to light the way for Aimless' soul-spirit during its walk along the path of souls, and to keep warm memories.

Luke sat beside the fire with Mutt next to him. He remembered that Aimless had wanted to live unknown and would want to stay that way. He wouldn't tell the authorities about the boy's murder. Before Luke stood up, he chanted a sacred song used in Chippewa ceremonies:

When the waters are calm and the fog rises,
I the spirit will now and then appear.

"Come on Mutt," he said leaving the burial site.

That night Luke camped just a day away from the border with Canada. He heated the last two packs of freeze-dried beef stew and shared them with Mutt. Before he crawled into his tent, he regarded the sky. Stars filled the emptiness with light. The constellation Orion, the hunter, shone strong.

THIRTY-FIVE

LUKE WAS ALONE when he reached Monument 78. He'd arrived later than the date he'd planned, and he had never felt more exhausted. But despite everything that had happened, he'd made it.

He touched the four-foot tall piece of granite. It was smooth and cold.

Luke set the timer on his camera. Then he stood next to the monument with a hand on Mutt's head. He waited for the timer to click down. He was unable to smile, but when he looked up into the tall trees, he was sure he saw Granddad nod.

At Manning Provincial Park, Luke had the lodge nearly to himself. The RCMP and press had left for Mazama, leaving a few unconcerned thru-hikers gathered in the restaurant and relaxing in the lodge's hot tub. Though they were unaware of what had happened a day earlier, Luke overheard them talking about some big incident on the trail. Rumors and news spread quickly up and down the trail.

The lodge accepted dogs for an extra $20.00. He collected Mutt, who waited outside, and hurried to his room to call

211

Marina. She'd be frantic by now. On the way, he bought a newspaper. The front page was covered with articles about the terrorist attempt. In one, FBI Director Mayberry stated that the FBI was aware of the terror network originating from Uktamiya, a radical movement in Kyrgyzstan. They had been monitoring the cell's movements, said the article, gathering as much intelligence as possible before bringing an attack to a sure halt. They also had waited until the last possible minute to gather criminal evidence for use in a trial of any terrorists captured.

Luke whacked the paper with his hand. *The FBI put this together fast.* He read further. Mayberry thanked the RCMP and other foreign intelligence services for their help and praised the cooperation between the countries. He said how grateful he was to the hard-working men and women of the FBI, other federal and local agencies, and the RCMP who were able to stop the attack. It went on and on.

Nothing changes, Luke thought, tossing the paper on the floor. *Almost nothing.*

He picked up the phone and called his home number.

EPILOGUE

MEDHI SIPPED HIS TEA. He scanned into the sky yet again, but there was no sign of his bird, Hassan. It was growing dark, too dark for pigeons to fly safely. Medhi was worried. And not because Hassan would be one of a dozen birds he planned to bring to the race in Lahore in a couple of weeks.

He heard a light knock at his door. He set aside his tea and walked down the steps that led from his rooftop to the street. It was Kamil, his friend and fellow pigeon fancier.

"Hello, Medhi. It's a lovely evening, no?"

"Yes, it is."

"I've just come by to see if you are ready to train a few birds tomorrow?"

"Yes, I remembered. I'll bring six or so to your house early."

"Good. We will take them in my cart beyond the hills."

"Fine. Fine. Thank you," said Medhi, turning to climb the stairs.

"Medhi, are you alright?" asked Kamil. "You seem anxious. Shall I sit with you a while?"

"Oh, no," answered Medhi. He rubbed his hands. "You know, it's just that my fingers are sore tonight. I worked very hard today."

"Ah, your carpets." Kamil smiled. "Your patterns are most intricate, Medhi, but you are not a young man. You must take it easy more."

"Thank you, my friend, you are right. I'll be fine to fly the birds tomorrow."

"Goodnight then, Medhi."

"Goodnight, Kamil."

"Oh, and Medhi?"

Medhi fought to keep his face calm. "Yes, my friend?"

"Remember to bring your fast one, Hassan. Isn't that his name?"

The mention of the bird's name brought a lump to his throat. "Yes, of course I'll bring him."

Medhi willed his friend to leave. When Kamil turned down the next street, he hurried back to the roof. He checked the loft, but Hassan was not there. Only his mate peering from her box.

Medhi returned to his chair. His tea had grown cold. The sun had set. It was too late for Hassan to return. Something had happened. A hunter might have shot him. Or perhaps a hungry falcon overtook him.

The air grew cool, but Medhi was unable to leave the roof.

He heard Hassan before he saw him. A light thump on the edge of the loft roof, then the pigeon's profile against the last slant of light.

Medhi's heart leapt as he watched Hassan push through the door into the loft and settle beside his mate.

He opened the loft door. "Hassan, Hassan," he whispered. He picked up the bird and looked him over carefully. He found no signs of a fight or bullet wound. "Whatever you encountered, you fought through. You are braver than a thousand lions."

His hand trembled as he removed the small aluminum capsule from the bird's leg. Before he returned Hassan to his box, he kissed the top of his head.

ELIZABETH MACALASTER hails from New England where she grew up among mountains, lakes, and the ocean, all of which fostered a love of nature. She studied biology at Goucher College and received Masters Degrees in Marine Biology and Science Journalism from Dalhousie University, NS, and Boston University. She's raised an octopus by hand and worked on a stern trawler in the North Atlantic assessing commercial fish stocks.

From scientist to science journalist, Elizabeth has focused on environmental and conservation issues. She worked as a writer/editor for the U.S. Department of the Interior and served as editor-in-chief for EPA's Chesapeake Bay Program in Annapolis, MD. With another author under their pen name, Ryan Ann Hunter, she's written award-winning children's books on technology and transportation, as well as a YA collection of stories about women spies.

Married to an FBI agent, Elizabeth and their two children lived all over the United States as her husband moved from post to post working in counterintelligence and counterterrorism programs. Her experience and inside knowledge of the FBI inspired her to write *Reckoning At Harts Pass*, her first novel.

She and her husband now share their time between Vermont and Maine where they are avid rowers and hikers.

217

CPSIA information can be obtained at www.ICGtesting.com
Printed in the USA
BVOW000752290313

316760BV00006B/14/P